The Last Love Letter 2

Warren Holloway

AMERICA'S NEW STORYTELLER

GOOD 2 GO PUBLISHING

The Last Love Letter 2

Written by Warren Holloway

Cover Design: Davida Baldwin – Odd Ball Designs

Typesetter: Mychea

ISBN: 978-1-947340-32-9

Copyright © 2018 Good2Go Publishing

Published 2018 by Good2Go Publishing

7311 W. Glass Lane • Laveen, AZ 85339

www.good2gopublishing.com

https://twitter.com/good2gobooks

G2G@good2gopublishing.com

www.facebook.com/good2gopublishing

www.instagram.com/good2gopublishing

The Last Love Letter

2

awn was just sitting down in her office at CDCC at 8:04 a.m. She was barely all there today, especially after the problematic night she ran into with her ex-fiancé fondling her while she was asleep. She could not stop crying in the shower because she wanted to be with Juan. She also wanted to tell him what had taken place. She needed to express her emotions to someone.

As she was in thought, she had the idea to keep Juan at the prison, so he would not get transferred.

She tapped the mouse on her computer and punched in her security code to access the files. She then went under Juan's employment status, noted as N/A, and changed it. She placed him in the kitchen staff dining hall, so she could at least see him every day on her lunch break.

Once she secured the employment, it seemed to take some of the stress off of her that she was feeling.

As she was closing out the file, the reception captain stuck his head in the office after briefly knocking.

"Here's our list for today. There are thirty-two from Philadelphia, a bunch of homicides and hard-asses."

"They all are until they come through here, stripped of everything—no guns and no gangs to back them," Dawn responded.

The captain made his way out of the office and left her to look over the files.

As she was looking at the papers, she was having a feeling of being watched, so she raised her head up, only to see Melanie looking back at her with a capricious and furtive look as if she was up to something.

Melanie still was not sure about Dawn and Juan, and a part of her thought that they were having more than a professional conversation, because she never saw Dawn call anyone from H-block.

Dawn also thought the same as Melanie, but vice versa. Dawn knew there was a reason why she mentioned Juan being on a visit. Dawn did not worry about it, because she knew she would get to the bottom of it.

Dawn focused back on her work. She did not want to have too many distractions taking her away from her job, a job she desperately needed to take care of her daughter, Breeana.

~ ~ ~

Juan was in his cell at 9:07 a.m. watching TV in H-block when he heard his name called over the intercom.

"Dominguez, you in?"

"Yeah, I'm here."

"You're starting in the kitchen today working in the officer's dining hall. Come down to the table. The runner has your kitchen whites."

The cell door buzzed open. He came out and made his way down to the table.

"Dominguez, right?" the block runner asked.

"Yeah. Where's the staff dining room at?"

"That's where you're working? Damn! You're going to see all the chicks," the block runner said. He then added, "It's at the end of the crosswalk. You make a left, but that's how the guards go in. You have to enter the main building unless you're with your supervisor."

"He said I start today, so what time?"

"Right now, their lunch starts at 9:00 a.m., but that's just for the guards. Then all the nurses and other administrative workers come in at 10:00 a.m., 11:00 a.m., and 12:00 noon. You get to eat well and see females."

"I can do that!" Juan said, thinking about seeing Dawn and Melanie.

Sergeant Stern came to the bubble window and tapped on the glass.

"Dominguez! Get dressed and come back down to see me, alright?"

"Yes, sir."

Juan ran up and got dressed, and he also made sure his breath smelled good and his hair looked perfect for all the females looking on.

He came back down to the bubble and climbed the short stairs to face Sergeant Stern, who wanted to give him a brief talk about working in the staff dining room.

"Dig this here, pretty boy! You going to be working around a lot of women: black, white, Puerto Rican. They're not for you to be lusting after or trying to get your mac on. Just serve the food and clean up, whatever it is they tell you to do. I don't want to have to rush over there to give you a few body shots to keep you in line, alright?"

"Yes, sir, I'm good. I touch in less than five months."

"Here's your pass. You know where you're going?"

"Yes, sir!"

Juan headed out the door and made his way to the walkway toward the dining hall. He could not wait to get to the staff dining hall.

When he walked into the main kitchen, the supervisor, Ms. Johnson, who was a short older Afro-American, came up to take his pass.

"Dominguez, I don't know who you know around here, but they put you in the staff dining room, which usually takes months or years to get in. You skipped right over the guys who have been waiting. Anyway, your job is to make sure the tables are clean, the trash is taken out, and the bathrooms are clean.

"Yes, ma'am. I won't let you down. I'll do a good job."

She gave a motherly smile, seeing that he was not about to fool around, but ready to work. Little did she know that Juan was a very suave individual.

"Follow me, Dominguez," Ms. Johnson said as she led the way into the staff dining room.

Some of the guards were already eating, while others were coming through the line. There were two other inmates inside the dining room behind the line serving the staff.

"Hey, Ms. J, who's the new guy?" Reggie B asked.

"This is Dominguez. His first name is Juan. Dominguez, this is Blassingale and Hosby."

"Call me Little Man. This is old head Reggie B a.k.a. Dead Eye," Little Man said.

Both were Afro-Americans working in the officer's dining hall for over a year.

"I'll leave him with you two. I already told him his duties, so don't try to give him anything extra," Ms. Johnson warned, giving them the eye as if she knew how they were when she was not around.

Once Ms. J walked away, they filled in Juan

on the layout of the workplace.

"Yo, cuz, I remember you from the paper with all that cash. You was doing your thing out there," Little Man said.

"A little something," Juan responded.

"Listen here, young buck. You look like you had a lot of women out there when you was home. But by now you should know you ain't home no more, but there is still a lot of women. Speak only if they speak, because some of them look down on us as if they too good and we they servants. Now you will get a few that are friendly, but it's just that. Don't let it go to your head, young buck."

"I got you, viejo."

Juan scanned the dining hall and saw that there were no cameras. He also checked out the bathroom area, which gave him an opportunity to get Dawn or Melanie by themselves to talk, kiss, or whatever.

Dead Eye was already making moves on a heavy-set nurse who was recently divorced and on the rebound. She found comfort in him, especially after seeing him five days a week. As for Little Man, he got one of the female guards pregnant. She was seven and a half months now and was taking time off. They still communicated via mail and phone.

While Juan was figuring out when he was going to see Melanie and Dawn and wondering if they took lunch at the same time, Deja was miles away just waking up in the sumptuous mansion of Tom Jones. She was lying naked with the satin sheets covering most of her body.

As her eyes fully opened, she reached out and found that Tom was not in bed.

"Papi, *adonde tu* papi?" she voiced, wondering where he was.

She slid out of the bed and dropped the sheet behind her as she made her way into the bathroom.

There was a note on the mirror with a single rose underneath it.

The note read: *Had to leave for Miami. Be back by dinner. You can stay if you want. Your car is in the garage. If you need anything, call me.*

She picked up the rose and smiled as she smelled it. She then closed her eyes and thought about the night before and then waking up to this.

After using the bathroom, she came out to the aroma of bacon, eggs, and toast. She knew Tom said he was out of town, but who was downstairs? she thought.

She looked around for her clothing, which was nowhere in sight. However, there was a robe lying on the side of the bed on the chair with another note that read: *You might need this until my assistant brings you something to wear.*

Another smile formed on her face. She loved how thoughtful he was.

She slipped on the robe to cover up her flawless body. She then made her way down the spiral staircase instead of taking the elevator. She followed the aroma of breakfast into the large kitchen.

When she walked inside, there was a female chef in her late thirties or early forties. She was of Italian-American background and stood five foot nine with blonde hair and grayish-green eyes.

"Good morning, Ms. Rodriguez," the chef said. "My name is Anita. I'm Mr. Jones's on-call chef. He said you might want to eat something before you start your day."

"It smells good in here," Deja said. "Do you know if his assistant came with the clothing?"

"She's on her way back now. She called right before you came down and wanted to know if you were awake yet," Anita continued. "You must be real special. Mr. Jones never has us do this for anyone other than family."

"I'll take that as a compliment from you and him," Deja responded, and this time her heart smiled.

"You are beautiful, and you just woke up. So, I can imagine how you look when you get dolled up."

"You are so sweet. Thank you."

Anita finished with the food. She then plated it and poured some freshly squeezed orange juice into a glass.

"Are you going to be eating down here or in the master suite?"

"I think I'll eat down here. I like talking to you; besides, you can tell me more about Tom," Deja said with a smile as she sat down.

The food looked as good as it smelled. Then Deja took a bite of the bacon and eggs and loved the taste of everything.

"Mmmmmmh, these are so good! Thank you for cooking."

"You're welcome. Now what do you want to know about Mr. Jones?"

"Has he ever been married or serious with any women before?"

"Never married. As for taking women seriously, he tried a few years ago, but that didn't work out. The girl got caught up spending his money, and not just on herself, but with other men. He discovered this when one of his workers spotted her out."

"That's a shame. I would never think of hurting him. Before I knew he had any of this, I thought he was sexy, attractive, and husband-type material, you know?" Deja said as she took another mouthful of eggs. "I don't need him to buy me things. It's nice, but I've been with someone that did that, and it made me gravitate toward him but for the wrong reasons. I see that looking back and being older now."

She was referring to Juan.

"I think you're a good choice for him. He's a busy man. You may be the one to slow him down and make him come home more, so he can appreciate all that he has—meaning the house and now you."

Deja was feeling good about what Anita was saying. It made her feel that she was being noticed by Tom's staff, who could see the true and genuine person she was.

Deja now needed to face severing her ties with Juan, if she wanted to give her all to Tom. She was prepared to ask another question, when Tom's assistant walked into the kitchen with her clothing.

"Good morning, everybody."

"Good morning, Brandy," Anita responded.

"*Bueno, mami.* I like your shoes," Deja responded.

"Then you'll like what I got you to wear today. Mr. Jones said you have style, so you can appreciate these True Religion jeans with the red Prada shirt and the shoes. I got two pairs to give you a choice, Cavalli or Dolce?"

"Brandy, you have good taste, but why would I dress up like that every day. That's a good outfit to go out in."

"If you don't like it, I can take it back. I picked out what Mr. Jones said you would like. Maybe he has something planned for you later on tonight?"

"You never know. He is full of surprises!" Anita added.

Tom had already given her an invitation to stay, but she thought she would have to go home for some clothing. However, she did not have to go in for work, since they were they were laying off people due to the economy, and she was one of them.

"If that's for tonight, then what shall I wear until then? I need to go to my place to get something comfortable to wear."

"What would you like?" Brandy asked.

Tom gave her specific orders to make sure Deja wanted for nothing, and also to make sure she was in the best of comfort.

"Sweats and a T-shirt. Something I can relax in."

"I have the perfect solution," Brandy said as she disappeared into the mansion.

She made her way up to the master suite and into the large walk-in closet that she helped arrange.

She picked out a pair of Tom's sweatpants and one of his Sean Jean T-shirts, and then headed back down to the kitchen.

"I figured I'd pull something from your

man's closet and give you a piece of him while he's away. It's also something comfortable, just as you requested."

Deja lit up inside and out. She loved how the ladies catered to her, thanks to Tom.

"Thank you, mami. You are so sweet."

"Deja, would you care for any more breakfast?" Anita asked.

"Let me get some more of that good bacon."

"Are you going to be eating here for lunch? If so, let me know what time, so I can prepare something."

"I just need to run home and secure a few things. Then I'll be back and wait for Tom to come home."

Brandy reached into her bag and pulled out a set of house keys.

"He must really trust his instincts about you,

because he asked that you take these if you're coming back."

Deja was falling for Tom by the second. Most men in his position would have had her leave before breakfast, or before he left town. This was the real thing. This was about building on something special—the road to a real love, which was something Juan was too immature to comprehend.

"*Gracias*, mami. I'll keep these close to me. It means a lot for him to believe in me like this. I am trustworthy. I just want to prove to him in the long run that what I bring to the table is real, and I'm all about him and for him."

"Don't worry, Deja. We got your back and his back. We'll let him know you're the real thing. We can see right through most people, and we see good in you," Anita said.

"Plus, you've got good taste," Brandy said. "So, I like you already; and your hair is real, so I don't have to buy any weaves for bad hair."

They all laughed knowing what she was talking about.

"I'm not even going to ask about that one," Deja said.

The ladies bonded and passed the time before Deja headed upstairs to freshen up for the day, so she could run home. She now knew she needed to sever all ties with Juan, which meant giving him his money, so he wouldn't have a reason to contact her.

Chapter 2

*D*awn took first lunch at 11:00 a.m. in the prison. She wanted to see Juan, and she hoped to get in a word with him, so she could feel good about standing her ground and being loyal to him after her ex-fiancé tried to move on her.

She walked into the staff dining room and up to the counter. She already knew the other two workers, Reggie and Little Man.

"Good morning, gentlemen. What do we have today?" she asked, referring to the meal.

"Cheeseburgers and fries. One of the many meals that we can't mess up!" Reggie B joked.

"I'll have that, but just a few fries. I'm going to get a salad too."

She grabbed her food and made her way over to a table in the corner by herself.

She scanned for Juan but did not see him until he exited the staff bathroom with a toilet brush and spray bottle of bleach in hand.

As he walked back to put the supplies away, he spotted her in the corner. When her eyes met his, the affection was felt at both ends. Her smile said it all. He knew that she was the one behind him getting the job and seeing her made having the job all worth it.

The glow she had as they made eye contact was special and different. He never experienced this type of emotional vibe, chemistry, or connection with Deja, or at least not on this mature of a level.

As he put back the supplies, Dawn continued to enjoy her food, knowing he would be the much-needed desert afterward.

There were only five people remaining in the dining hall. Juan walked over to Dawn's table to check and see if she needed anything. He also grabbed her tray.

"You look different but good this morning," Juan said in a low tone.

She did look and feel different for a reason— and he was the reason.

"I'm happy to see you. It's like you're my fix, so I'm all better now," she said in a baby-like voice, which made him feel her vibe even more.

"We'll get a chance to see one another Monday through Friday, which will allow us to build on the promising future we both want."

Reggie B and Little Man were behind the counter looking over at Juan. They both wondered why it was taking him so long to get the tray and ask her what she needed.

"Young buck, you good over there? You need help with something?" Reggie B asked, not knowing Juan was secretly taking care of business.

Juan grabbed the tray and stared into Dawn's eyes at the same time.

"I'll be right back."

She wanted to smile but held it back since the attention was directed in their area.

"I got everything, viejo. She just saw that I was the new guy, so she was running it down to me about how inmates get caught up. Basically, the same shit you was talking."

"My fault, young buck. I ain't mean to blow up your spot like that."

"You good. She just needed another soda," Juan lied.

Little Man filled the glass of Cherry Coke with no ice, just as she always requested.

"Here you go, cuzo."

Juan headed back to the table with the glass in hand.

"One Cherry Coke for the beautiful lady."

She giggled knowing he pulled it off with his co-workers.

"They were being nosey and not thinking I could do my job. I'm not going to stay long talking because I know they're watching me."

Dawn looked over at the counter, and they were looking back.

"You're right, baby. They are staring. I'll write you tonight."

"You should be getting something in the mail."

"You too," she added as he walked away.

Juan made his rounds to the other tables, making sure the staff did not need anything. He also made it look like he was flowing with the work.

Juan stood watching a few more staff members exit as some more came in. Some of them mingled with Reggie B and Little Man. The nurse that Reggie was into walked in with a smile from the entrance all the way to the counter, and Juan took note. He knew what that smile was about, since he saw the same expression in Dawn. He just did not know who it was for, until she spoke.

"Good morning, Mr. B."

Her voice was full of love and passion as if she was talking to her husband. Reggie was her new love. Juan picked up on this quickly since her entire demeanor changed.

"The morning is going well. Life is even better seeing you," he said in a friendly manner, just in case someone else heard and took it the wrong way.

Once she was served her food, she walked over to a table, with Reggie right behind her.

"I got her tray, young buck," he said, strolling from behind the counter.

Juan chuckled since he knew what was happening. This also gave him the opportunity to make eye contact with Dawn.

Her eyes were smiling, especially when he nodded his head toward the bathroom area, where there was a secluded 10' x 8' area away from the dining area.

She started off first. Juan gave her a thirty-second head start before he began to move his feet in that direction.

His heart pounded and butterflies stirred in his stomach the closer he got to the bathroom area. She was also excited, and her belly was also full of butterflies. Her heart throbbed for his comfort, and her body yearned to be held by him. She so wanted his touch.

She entered the area first, standing with her back against the wall. She took in a deep breath. She knew how risky this was, but the intrigue of the situation was gravitating and pulled her in by the second. They were getting away with something that they were not supposed to be doing, but it felt so good and so right, no matter how wrong it was.

He turned left into the area and saw her against the wall. Words did not need to be exchanged. She pulled him close for a passionate kiss. It was random, and he did not expect it. The kiss was unique and full of passion, yet it ignited emotions within both of them as it soared through their bodies. Their hearts pounded, and their hands moved across each other's bodies. She felt soft to him while his body felt firm and muscular to her. It was the comfort she wanted. The kiss also stimulated their bodies, and she could feel his stiffness, which made her heat up. She loved what was taking place inside and outside of her body, but she needed to bring control to herself and the situation.

She pushed him away a little and unlocked her lips. Words were still not spoken, but their eyes spoke to one another as they sparkled.

"I really need you in my life, Juan," she said affectionately, breaking the silence. "Just make sure you'll be good here and come home."

She did not even give him a chance to respond. She leaned in to kiss him once more, briefly but passionately. She then composed herself before walking back to her table, leaving him standing stiffly with the thought of the words she just had told him.

He snapped back to reality when he heard Sergeant Stern's voice boom through the air.

"Dominguez! Where's he at?" he yelled as he strolled over to the vending machine to get a bag of Middlesworth chips.

Juan came out from the bathroom area composed and focused.

"What's up, Serg?"

"Nothing, I'm just checking up on you, playa, and making sure you're doing your job since you got this out of the blue."

Reggie B came over to save Juan from the

sergeant's full-court press.

"He good, Stern. Plus, he's a hard worker."

"Alright. My man say you good, so I'ma take his word."

Sergeant Stern knew Reggie B from the streets. The sergeant was only there taking a short break. He just wanted to patronize Juan in the process.

Timing was everything, and Juan and Dawn ended their kiss and brief talk just in time.

Juan stood back over by the counter as Dawn was finishing her lunch, looking even sexier to him now. Her glow was also brighter, and the affection permeated through her body. She was feeling the much-needed comfort she yearned for since last night.

She gathered her things before she looked back and made eye contact with Juan. Her eyes were still smiling, but not her face. She wanted to keep their sub rosa life just between them.

~ ~ ~

About fifteen minutes passed by before Melanie came through the doors talking with one of her female nurse friends she knew from high school. She was so wrapped in her conversation that she did not even notice Juan at first, but her girlfriend spotted him.

"Looks like we have some new guy working here, and he's cute. Too bad he's on lockdown. I guess that's where all the good men are," Danika said.

Melanie zoomed in on the new guy and immediately saw that it was Juan. She started fixing herself up as if she was ready to go on a date with him.

Little Man and Reggie did not like the two

women. They always seemed to have their heads high as if they were above them.

"These are the type of chicks we was talking about. Don't say shit to them," Little Man suggested.

Danika walked up to the front of the line and smiled at Juan until Melanie nudged her. She then batted her eyes at him before speaking.

"Good morning."

Reggie B and Little Man looked at Juan and wondered what was going on. How was he able to get them to check him out and speak?

"Yes, it is a good morning."

After Melanie and Danika sat down at their table, Juan waited a few seconds before walking over to pick up their trays.

"Let me know if you two need anything else. I'm the new guy, Juan or Dominguez. Whatever you choose to call me."

Danika was still checking him out, thinking to herself what fun she would have with him if they crossed paths on the outside. Melanie saw her leering at him and did not like it one bit, which made her take mental note not to eat lunch with her again.

"Thank you, Juan. You're nicer than the other guys," Melanie joked.

Juan walked away and allowed the ladies to enjoy their lunch. He also did not want to have a conversation with Melanie while her friend was there.

Five minutes passed before Danika got up from the table. She had to call her babysitter to check in on her kids, using the pay phone in the staff dining room. Juan grabbed his supplies and headed toward the bathroom area, where

Melanie's eyes followed. She followed him a few seconds later. She wanted another kiss like when she crossed him in the visiting area.

The only staff members remaining in the dining hall at this time were all females, so he entered the men's room to clean it up.

Melanie did not see which bathroom he entered, only that he went in that area. She first stuck her head into the women's bathroom, but no Juan, so she entered the men's bathroom much to his surprise.

"Hey, you!" she said as she walked into the bathroom and startled him.

"What are you doing in here? You're crazy!"

"I may be, but there's something about you that drives me crazy," she said while moving in for a kiss.

He did not resist her advance, remembering

how she was the day before. She was also aggressive. Her hands roamed his body, touching his manhood and feeling the rise of his power.

"I masturbated last night thinking about you and the kiss," she said in a low, sexual, panting voice.

Her words turned him on even more. Now his hands pressed against her breasts, which caused her to send a light moan into his ears.

He was hard and horny. He had not had sex in a long while since he was on lockdown. He did not know if she would make the move toward sex, but then again, he could not do this to Dawn. She respected herself a little more, but she was in control of herself a little more too.

He pressed his fingers against her love spot and rubbed the outside of her pants. She sighed. "Ooh, I want you!"

Juan stopped right then and took a good look at her. He was processing his thoughts on what was about to happen.

"We only have a few minutes!" he said, leaving the decision up to her.

"Okay," she responded.

She quickly unbuttoned her pants and pulled them down, before bending over with her hands touching the counter.

Juan was already stiff. He came up behind her and grabbed her soft, warm ass. He pressed himself inside of her tightness. It was so good, and he thought he was going to lose it. His heart raced, and the excitement of the situation and getting caught only added to it. She looked at him in the mirror as he went in and out, hitting every spot and making her moan.

"Ohhhhh, mmmmmh! Ohhhhhh shit!" she

screamed as she came from the rush of butterflies soaring through her, plus his stiffness filled her love spot and touched all of her.

Juan's movement picked up. He wanted to finish, because he loved how she felt to him. He slammed harder and harder into her love spot. Her eyes connected with his as she released the uncontrollable sensation that he was causing her body to feel. Then he exploded inside of her, something she loved, because it made her release even more.

Juan removed himself only to hurry up and wipe down. She did the same, using the towels with which he came into the bathroom to clean.

"How do I look?" she asked, after quickly fixing herself up before leaving the bathroom.

"Satisfied and happy!" He laughed.

"That was good. Better than anything I ever had, which only added to the excitement of where we are at."

"You're a freak—an exhibitionist."

"You too, since I didn't do it by myself. Just wait until you come home. We can do it everywhere," she said as she leaned in to kiss him before walking out.

Juan was in a place most inmates would never be. He had something and someone as good as her and Dawn on his side.

Melanie was satisfied for the moment, but she wanted more of Juan. She wanted his love, and she wanted all of him. She did not want anyone else to have him either. Whether she knew it or not, she was one up on Dawn. By sexing Juan in the bathroom, she was heavy on his mind, body, and heart right now.

Chapter 3

*D*eja was just walking into her apartment in Harrisburg at 12:33 p.m., which was a big difference from Tom's place, but it was her own space. The space was filled with photos and memories of Juan and the relationship they once had. She could not help the stirring of emotions that came over her for her feelings she had for both Tom and Juan. But it was more of letting Juan down and turning her back on him once again. Tears slid down the side of her face as she walked through the apartment toward the bedroom to retrieve Juan's money, which she kept in the same Nike shoebox he had it in.

She dumped the money on the bed and counted it out. She cried and wished she had never spent his money, so he could have it all when he returned home. She especially felt guilty that he would no longer be coming home to her, because she was now chasing her true romance and happy ending with Tom.

Only $37,000 remained from the initial $150,000.

She secured rubber bands around all of the money, keeping it as Juan would like to see it. She wiped away her tears and placed the remaining block of money into the box. She then lay in the middle of her bed crying and thinking about her new life, new things, and a new person. It was dream-like, and she hoped that she would not get hurt. But she also thought that there is a risk in everything, especially finding true love.

She got up from the bed and walked around

the apartment taking down all of Juan's pictures. She then returned to the letter with his name on it that she originally ignored when she entered the apartment. She did not want to read the letter because she knew how his words could pull her back. Although she attempted to set it back down, a part of her wanted to hear what he had to say.

She scanned the letter, picking out certain parts, when something caught her eye. She paused from reading the letter and covered her mouth as another tear slid down her face.

It read: *Just know when the money is gone, love will still be here. Love can't be spent; however, it can be wasted if it's not appreciated.*

As she read this, she could hear his voice saying the words.

Maybe he was right, but it did not mean his love was for her. She struggled with these thoughts, before heading back into her bedroom to grab the writing tablet and pen. She would write him a heartfelt letter, something she hoped he would understand and appreciate one day.

Once the letter was finished, she made her way into the bathroom and fixed her makeup since she had cried it off. When she was done, she grabbed the money and letter and then walked outside to her car. She dropped off the letter in the mailbox by the development exit.

As she pulled out of the complex and headed back to Tom's place, her cell phone sounded off.

She did not get a chance to see who it was. She quickly answered it, since she did not want to look down while she was driving.

"Hello."

"Good afternoon, sexy."

She knew the voice. It was Tom on the other end of the phone. Hearing his voice made her feel good all over again, and it allowed her to know she was doing the right thing and heading in the right direction with him.

"Damn, papi! You could have woken me up this morning, so I could have seen your pretty-boy face and given you a few kisses before you left."

"Don't worry, I kissed you a few times while you were sleeping peacefully and making it look good at the same time. I didn't want to disturb what looked like art or perfection." He laughed.

"Mmmmmh! So, when you coming back, papi?"

"Before dinner. Speaking of which, did you

meet Brandy and Anita?"

"Yes, they are so nice and good at what they do."

"So, did you like what Brandy got you?"

"The question is, would you like to see me in it or out of it when you come home?"

Tom had to laugh. He loved her playful side, which was sexy and interesting at the same time.

"How about I watch you get dressed, piece by piece, starting from the tub water beads racing down your body, to the towel drying you off. I want to see your panties slide up your legs and fit snug on your flesh, comfortably fitting every curve. Then the same with the bra as they cover up perfection."

He was flowing with his words and placing her in the moment, almost seeing him watching her.

"You make it sound so good and dream-like."

"That's what I was trying to do. It's the best way to build on a relationship, keeping it sexy, so we can always appreciate one another."

Juan's words flashed into her mind when he said, "Appreciate one another." This made her realize that she was not doing a bad thing; she was simply following her heart.

"I think with you I'll always find a reason to appreciate you and what you do for me and our relationship."

"As long as we keep the newness, that good vibe we feel right now. If we keep that going, then falling in love and staying in love will be easy."

Her heart was fluttering at his every word. She was emotionally open to him right now. Thus far, he knew how to make her heart, mind, and body smile. What more could a woman ask for?

"I'm looking forward to this life of love you speak of, papi. I hope you know that I'm all you need, and you'll be all I want!"

"My instincts tell me I made a good decision with you, so let's make the best of it by building this house of love, a place where you and I will always feel at home."

A tear formed in the corner of Deja's eye, but this time it was a happy tear—a tear of feeling compassion.

"You make me happy, papi," she said.

"I hope you say this ten years from now, instead of 'you get on my nerves, papi.'" he said, being funny and making her laugh.

Since he heard her voice break a little, he wanted to cheer her back up.

"You are so stupid, but you make me laugh, which is good, papi."

Deja could hear male voices in the background calling for Tom to finish up on the meeting.

"Deja, as you can see, I need to finish up with this meeting. We were discussing financial plans to have a Legacy Rentals down here in Miami, and also one of my restaurants."

"Good luck, papi. I'll see you later, okay?"

"I'm looking forward to it, beautiful," he said before hanging up.

She was on cloud nine and back on track emotionally. She headed to her mom's house in uptown Harrisburg, so she could fill her in on the new man of hers, which was something she had not done since she was with Juan.

Deja's mom never liked Juan anyway, because he was arrogant and flashy and was not a hard-working man like her husband. She did not respect drug dealers.

Deja's mom lived on McClay Street, which was two doors from the Lucky 7 bar. She parked her car across the street in Edmont Plaza in front of Chan's Chinese restaurant.

Her mom was sitting out front in her chair with her cousins that were playing cards, smoking cigarettes, and drinking beer from the bar next door.

The music was playing, and the aroma of Latino soul food was in the air coming from inside the house.

As she approached, her mom stood up to hug her baby girl.

"*Ahi Dios mio, mi hija.* I haven't seen you in weeks. Where have you been, nena?" she asked with open arms. "*Dame un abrazo!*"

Deja gave her mom a big hug.

"*Adonde, papa?*" Deja asked.

"*En la casa con amigos.*"

Deja's mom, Carmen, knew something was either wrong or her baby girl needed to tell her something. It was not only a mother's instinct, but Deja was also playing with her hair, which was something she did as a child when something was bothering her, or she needed to express something.

"*Que pasa, nena?*" Carmen asked, making eye contact as she patted on the seat beside her. "*Asiento, nena, habla con me.*"

Deja sat down, placed her arm around her mother, and then laid her head on her shoulder.

"It's over between me and Juan for good. I had to let him go, Ma."

"Don't worry, nena, he was no good for you. You'll find a good man like Papi, and then you'll be happy."

"I did, Ma. I found someone," she said, raising up her head to make eye contact with her.

"*Quien es ese?*"

"*Moreno*, Tom Jones. He's a good man, and he treats me good, Ma."

Carmen could hear it in her daughter's voice that she found the right one, because this is how she sounded when Deja's father treated her like that.

"I don't care about you dating a moreno. It is your father you need to worry about. I believe if you find love, or the right person, you don't see race, nena. You only see happiness."

"I think papa will like him. He's a hard-working businessman, and he treats me good emotionally."

"When are you going to bring him around, so your father can talk to him, so he can make sure he is a real man as you say?"

"I'll talk to him about this at dinner tonight. He's in Miami on business right now."

Deja was happy, and that was all that was important to her mother. Now she needed to go speak to her father.

"I'm going to talk to papa before I leave," she said as she got up and made her way inside.

Deja's presence got the attention of everyone in the house. Her father's friends stopped playing dominos when they all saw the beautiful Deja standing in front of them with a smile.

"*Ven aqui, mi hija,*" her father said.

She walked over and gave him a hug.

"I haven't seen you in awhile. Is everything okay?"

"Yes, I was just dropping by to make sure you and ma are doing fine. I also let her know I'm not with Juan anymore."

"*Bueno, bueno*! So, who is the new guy, *mi hija*?"

"His name is Tom Jones."

Deja's father, Carlito, had heard the name Tom Jones before. He had seen billboards advertising Legacy Rentals, and he also saw Tom on television donating money to the black and Latino communities to rebuild houses.

"I know this name from TV and advertisement. He's a good man to the people."

"He's also a good man to me, papa," she said, lighting up with a smile.

Carlito would do anything to keep his baby

girl happy, but he still wanted to meet Tom to have a face-to-face man talk.

"When do I get to meet this Tom Jones?"

"*Yo no se.* But I told ma that I'll talk to him tonight about this."

"Okay, whatever makes you happy, princess."

"Thank you, Papa. I love you so much," she said as she hugged him once more before exiting the house. "Ma, I'll talk to him. He says he knows who he is but wants to speak with him."

Carmen was happy for her daughter. She was on the right path to a relationship that would not have the strain of prison to interrupt it or test its love.

Deja hugged her mom once more before heading off to Tom's place to get rested and ready for the night.

Chapter 4

Juan was in his cell at 3:31 p.m. opening the letter that Dawn had sent him. He immediately noticed the picture of Breeana, along with her innocence, young beauty, hazel eyes, and warm smile. It made him realize the commitment he would now have to accept. This was a real relationship with a real little girl. He set the picture to the right of the letter as he opened it up to read it.

Dear Juan:

It took a lot for me to get to this point of wanting to trust someone again, let alone in the position you're in. I'm trusting with my heart that you'll be good to me; but keep in mind, if you hurt me, you hurt my daughter. Because being in a relationship with me, my daughter will get to meet you, and you will be a part of her life, because you're a part of her mommy's life. Juan, I think about you and a future with you all of the time. This is how I know in my heart, mind, and body that what we're doing is right. Love is possible in this position. We can get to know each other's secrets and the most intimate things that will allow you and I to grow into something special as you stated. Just don't play with my emotions or my life. What I mean is, don't waste my time with game or games. If you can be honest, and be about me and this relationship, then the future I fantasize about all of the time with you will come true. With that said, baby, take care. I can't wait to see you.

Respectfully,

Dawn

After Juan finished reading the letter, he glanced over at Breeana's picture and took it all in. He was thinking about the kiss with Dawn and how passionate it was, as well as the words she left him with before walking away. She needed him in her life. They were words of commitment and of someone wanting it all—the perfect love story.

Juan wanted the same ending; however, he felt selfish for his desperate act with Melanie, and it was a tortuous situation. Although he gravitated toward Melanie for her aggressiveness and good traits, he felt the same way with Dawn and her wife qualities. He felt something for the both of them.

He took his pen, flipped to a blank page on his tablet, and released his thoughts and emotions on paper to Dawn.

The Perfect Love Story

LOVE, a deep affection or fondness . . . sexual pleasure that could lead to promises. A promise is commitment or assurance that someone will undertake action . . . "Lights, cameras, action," a love story is in motion, so envision yourself being chosen, picture the place, the perfect person and the moment, and then own it . . .

Capture the romance and embrace that one chance to fall in love again. That's love with no pain, no emotional strain, nothing to hold you down. That's the past, and you've been released from those chains . . . This is a love story, and you're the star, the writer, producer, and director, so when it comes to your emotions, it's like GEICO, you're protected . . . The portrait-like love is priceless, dreamlike as the white sands feel warm on your feet as the stars in the sky are bright and wishes can be made. But your one wish is right beside you, the man of your dreams; your second wish is for him always to know what to do and say; and the third is for this love story to have a happy and perfect ending.

Written with passion by Juan Dominguez

He set down his pen and turned to the window in thought, flashing into the future with Dawn. He could see himself walking into the house, feeling welcome, seeing her face, and being greeted by a kiss filled with as much or even more passion than the kiss he shared with her today. Little Breeana would race up to him, ready to show him the dessert she helped Mommy make for him. The rest of the day would include dinner and then a movie, their warm bodies permeating with love for one another. He would listen to how her day went in between kisses to her soft lips, and he'd get to see her priceless smile after exchanging the words "I love you."

Juan was in deep thought until the intercom sounded off.

"Five minutes 'til count! Five minutes!" The yelling officer brought him back to the reality of where he was.

Juan wrote a brief letter to Dawn to compliment the poem, before he then he moved on to writing Melanie.

Mel B:

What up, sexy? I can't believe we made it happen in

the bathroom today. I wish I had more time to make love to you, because this is what you deserve, although the excitement of our environment made it interesting. You gave me a part of you, and it says a lot. I want to follow my instincts and heart when I write and speak to you, because it's the right thing to do. Also, I want to make you happy—the luckiest woman in the world if possible.

Mel, you should be getting some more money soon. I want to keep my promise from that end to make sure you stay happy. Not that money is everything, because without it, we still can establish something beautiful called love.

Think about my words and don't just read them. Allow them to connect with you on an emotional and mental level and allow them to show you belief. Right now, we have to live in secret, but when I get there, we can show off this good thing that we've become, and then show off our love. I say "love" because I know being with you it will come. You'll make falling for you easy. Just keep in mind, the same way you got me is the same way you keep me.

Mel, I'm going to close this for now by adding a poem

to connect with you. I also hope it will place a smile on your heart and face.

One love, Juan

Juan could not help but fall right back into his insidious ways, since he was not being mature enough to be with just one person. A part of him wanted to have both, but the reality of it all was he could only be with one woman and make her happy by doing so. Both Dawn and Melanie deserved to have the best and be happy. He was in a position of playing his cards until the end to see who would be the last standing of the two, which was something that most incarcerated men did.

Juan did not want to be alone. He did not want to be broke, and he did not want to break either of the females' hearts. These were a few of his fears. He had control over all of them, but he did not act as if he did.

"Count time! Count time! Count time!" the loud voice of the officer boomed over every intercom in the cells as well as over the block area, making sure everyone heard the call for standing count.

Juan and his cellmate, Puto, stood up. After the guards passed by, Juan got back to his writing. He was sending a poem with the letter he wrote for Melanie.

Keeping A Secret

I can keep a secret; however, seeing you expose my weakness I get weak when my heart is taken by your presence. It is powerful, yet pleasant . . . sweetness fills the air, your scent. I have to admit, I'm easily lured by your eyes, and wanting to be close, wanting to feel the warmth and the softness of your lips . . . A little taste of pleasure is appeasing to the mental, but it's your heart and your mind that I would love to get into. I'm so intrigued to know what's on the menu. A real woman driven by her own means is compassionate and full of love, shaking the pain. It's been awhile since real love, and you're ready to be treated like a queen . . . I can keep a secret, and we can be more than friends and build on something our hearts believe in . . . I'm a simple man, so I don't ask for much. We can make this exciting, kind of like a teenage crush. When you pass by me, no one needs to know or notice, yet we get those butterflies and that rush.

Written with passion by Juan

~ ~ ~

Melanie was at her apartment in New Cumberland at 4:34 p.m. just finishing up a number one from McDonald's, a meal she grabbed on the way home from work. She did not feel like cooking. Her focus was writing Juan about the exciting day she had. She wanted more of him, and her emotions were becoming involved faster than she expected.

Melanie lived in a one-bedroom apartment furnished with a green leather couch and loveseat that her parents got her as a house-warming gift, oak wood coffee and end tables, and neutral carpeting throughout. Her bedroom had a king-size bed, black furniture, and a mirror backdrop in the headboard. The apartment also boasted a small dining room area off the kitchen, where her small bar-like table sat with four high chairs.

Melanie saw that she had received a letter from Juan, which placed a smile on her face and made her reflect back to the bathroom action.

She opened his letter and read it, and then she read it again to absorb all of his words and visualize him speaking to her. Reading the letter accompanied by what took place at work that day made her feelings for Juan even more enhanced. She did not just want more of him sexually; she wanted him emotionally as well.

She sat at the dining room table writing out

a brief letter, before she made her way into the bathroom to bathe.

Hey amigo:

I just finished reading your letter from the kiss in the visiting hallway. It was special, and your words meant a lot in the letter, just as you're starting to mean something to me. I know this money thing started this relation-ship, but I hope that we can continue outside of prison as well as outside the money thing. I want you to take me seriously. Don't think because of what we did in the bathroom that I'm not a good girl, because I am. I did this for you. No one else is getting a part of me—only you. I want you to have a part of my heart just as you did my body. I want you in my life, so we can have exciting moments like today. Things like today are how we'll keep the fire in our relationship. Well, let me know if you really feel the same. I think you do from reading your letter; I just hope it's real. Well, amigo, I can't wait to see you tomorrow.

Sincerely,

Mel B

As she folded the letter and placed it in the envelope, she thought about Juan with a smile on her face. She set the letter down where she would remember to pick it up and mail it in the morning.

Melanie walked toward the bathroom while stripping out of her work clothing and placing them in the hamper outside the bathroom. She then turned on the hot water and added vanilla and rose-scented bubble bath as she watched the bubbles form and smelled the aroma filling the air.

The doorbell rang followed by a knock at the door, just as her tub was filled to her liking. She was not expecting any visitors. Her friends usually called before they came over.

When she arrived at the door and looked out the peephole, she saw that it was Juan's friend,

Deja, the same girl she had seen hugging and kissing Juan.

She opened the door with a vacuous smile.

"Hi."

"How are you doing, Melanie?"

"I'm good. What brings you here today?" she asked, not remembering Juan saying anything about her coming over.

"I have something for you. Can I come in?"

"Sure, come in," Melanie welcomed her into the living room. "You can take a seat, if you don't mind."

Deja sat down and pulled out the rubber band with $5,000 around it. Although she did not want to give Melanie the money, since she had already spent much of it, it was the least she could do before walking away from Juan.

"He asked me to give you another $5,000."

She set the money on the coffee table.

Although Melanie was happy to see the cash, she knew that there was something else.

"I sent him a letter to let him know I'm done, so he is going to have to figure out who he's going to get to bring you the money from now on."

"Thank you for dropping this off. I just finished reading his letter. I hope he acts right when he comes home, because I really want us to work, you know?" Melanie said, being slick with her wording and making sure Deja knew that she was in Juan's life outside of the money situation. "He's so sweet the way he talks about having the perfect love, and building on something special."

A part of Deja wanted to jump up and leave because she was just breaking it off with Juan, but it did not mean she did not still have feelings for him. Instead, she smiled with the thought that Melanie would learn someday.

Hearing this also allowed Deja to realize that she was making the right decision, which was following her heart to be with Tom, a real man.

"It sounds like you two have it all figured out," Deja said as she stood up from the couch.

"I hope so. I've been single for a while, and our infatuation with one another makes it feel like we have a teenage crush."

Deja shook her head as she made it to the door, where she saw the letter Melanie was sending to Juan, which made it all too real for her. Now she did not feel bad for letting him go.

Deja left without saying goodbye. Melanie knew she had struck a nerve, just as she did with Dawn in the office. She wanted to make sure no one had a chance to be with Juan other than her.

Melanie closed the door and made her way back to the bathroom where her hot bubble bath awaited. She slipped out of the robe that she put on before answering the door and then stepped into the hot, soothing tub.

She leaned her head back and took a deep breath. Her mind flashed between the excitement of her and Juan in the bathroom to the future with him. In her images of the future, they had a family. He was a good father and loving husband. He played with the kids but also found time to play with her and make her laugh and love him even more.

She could feel his hands massage her body after a long day of work, with his hands pressing deep into her flesh to relax her in every way. While the kids slept, the massage turned into deep, passionate, and intimate love-making, which was something they both appreciated. She put her mouth on his neck to muffle the moans as not to wake the kids. Her love bites stimulated the moment as their hearts pounded from the intense passion yet beat as love was being made.

Melanie opened her eyes and felt her fingers caressing herself. Just as she was near climax, she closed her eyes again. This time she flashed to the action in the bathroom with his stiffness, the excitement, and the rush of getting caught. She was turned on by it all and moaned. With her mouth open and sighing in pleasure, she could feel him inside her all over again as her body continued to erupt in pleasure.

Deja's face flashed into her image at the last second, which brought a sadistic smile to Melanie's face. It was as if Deja was watching her with Juan, which turned her on even more. She knew she got what Deja no longer had or wanted to have at one point.

Chapter 5

D awn was at her place in Mechanicsburg at 6:38 p.m. reading Juan's letter for the third time and finding herself emotionally wrapped in his words that were customized for her, especially the poem "I Won't Forget." It made her embrace what she was building with him. He knew what to say and how to say it in order to make her feel the affection and comfort of his words and his presence. Each time she read the letter, she paused afterward to reflect back on the kiss. It was full of emotion. Her body and heart loved each second. His lips were soft, and his tongue moved in and out of her mouth tasting like a starlight mint. His hands roamed her body and made her feel like she was melting in his grasp. The thought alone made her giggle and laugh each time.

She was feeling reborn in finding this new relationship with Juan. Her heart was guiding her in the right direction while falling in love and finding a love that would also appreciate her at all times, and even accept her daughter as part of the package.

She set the letter down, reached for the glass of red wine on the coffee table, and took a sip. It was her third glass. She was celebrating her newfound love, a promising future, and a life of happiness.

Breeana was in her room winding down for the night watching her favorite cartoons. Dawn was having some quiet alone time as well. It was her way to relax with a drink and think about Juan to the point where his presence felt so real.

Now she had more to go on. His touch and his kiss made her visions of him more tangible.

She cuffed the pillow after finishing off the third glass of wine and then leaned into the corner of the plush couch. She closed her eyes thinking about Juan, her true love. A smile formed on her face as she snuggled into the pillow that she was embracing as if it was Juan himself. She was in her place of comfort: Romanticville.

In her thoughts, Juan walked into the apartment over to her. She could feel his presence and his warm body as he kissed her cheek.

"Get up, beautiful. Tomorrow's our big day," she heard him say.

She opened her eyes and saw a smile on his face as he grabbed her left hand to kiss it. She felt the softness and warmth of his lips press against her hand.

When his lips pulled away from her hand,

she noticed the flawless, three-carat diamond engagement ring on her finger. Her heart pounded for his love upon seeing this. She was getting married, something she always wanted.

Her images skipped to the big day where she was standing beside him all in white, with butterflies in her stomach and love in her heart. This was it, the moment she was waiting for.

She turned to him and saw his glow. He was happy, and she was in love. The vows were exchanged, and her heart was now complete. They were one, and she was Mrs. Dominguez.

Dawn was far into her fantasy dream state, falling in love and opening her emotions to Juan even more, whether she knew it or not.

After the wedding and honeymoon, she envisioned somewhere special. It was a resort with rose petals from the front door to a bubble bath and then to the bed. Juan planned this all out, which was so thoughtful of him, she felt. His gestures made her love and appreciate him even more.

The large bathroom boasted his-and-hers sinks, a jet shower, and marble features with gold fixtures. Lingerie set the tone, where she kept it sexy wearing royal-blue lace that complemented her red hair.

She exited the bathroom and approached the bed where Juan awaited her. She could hear his voice speaking to her.

"*Tu sonrisa es bonita*, nena."

She loved when he spoke Spanish to her. It was a romantic language, and even more poignant when in love with the person speaking it.

She looked down at her wedding band and diamond engagement ring. She loved them both, just as much as the man before her. She then climbed onto the bed with a salacious loving look in her eyes. She was ready to reward her husband for loving her the way he did.

She began kissing his legs and making her way up to his manhood, which was standing firm. Her feminine hand took hold of him and slowly made him feel good. Then her lips followed, where she kissed his love stick with smiles that sent pleasure to him. She worked her magic and then paused. She wanted him inside. She wanted him to make love to her. He grabbed her by the waist, removed the blue lace lingerie, and kissed her belly button at the same time, which sent pleasure through her body.

After tossing the lingerie to the side, she slid down on him, moaning and loving how he felt. She worked her hips as his hands gripped her side to assist the motion while hanging on for the ride. Their eyes connected, and the love could be seen. She then halted her motion and flipped over to her back. She wanted to be closer and more intimate. He embraced her by pulling her close to kiss as he moved passionately. This was love-making, she thought. This is how she wanted it. She could feel her body heating up. The tingling sensation rushed and soared through her body with his every movement. Her mouth opened, and she erupted with pleasure. Her heart was falling further into love, and she loved everything about this man.

Dawn was in her fantasy dream state living out the life she wanted with Juan. She hoped real life with Juan would be just the same.

Chapter 6

A t 7:35 p.m., Tom and Deja pulled up to Sakura on Carlisle Pike. The Japanese restaurant was one of Tom's favorites, even before he was wealthy. This was the place he came to when he would have a good week selling cars and before buying them to rent. As soon as they entered the restaurant, he was recognized by a server who was dressed as a Geisha minus the makeup.

"Mr. Jones, glad to have you back. Would you like to sit at the bar or in a private booth?"

"A booth would be fine."

"Follow me, sir."

Once they arrived in their private booth, the server took their drink orders and then placed menus in front of them.

"Have you ever eaten sushi before, Deja?"

"No, but I have had octopus in a salad. You know I'm a Latina, papi. We eat good too."

"The best thing about the sushi here is it's so fresh. If you need any help ordering, just let me know."

"I'm going to get the octopus and squid sashimi, the mussels, and a dragon roll."

"Sounds good, baby."

"It looks good in this picture, too, papi."

The server returned with the drinks, cucumber salads, and chopsticks. She was ready to take their order.

"Are you ready to order, or do you need more time, Mr. Jones?"

"I think we're ready."

Deja ordered the same thing she said she was going to order.

"I'll have a TNT roll, a spicy number 10, an order of mussels, two spicy tuna wraps, and a spicy number 5."

"Will that be all?"

"For now!"

Once the server left, Deja commented on his order.

"So, you like everything hot and spicy, papi?" she asked with her eyes smiling.

"I do have the privilege of having the sexiest and spiciest thing from Puerto Rico—that being you."

"Mmmmh, so you like the way I taste, huh?"

"Wow, you crazy! But, yes, if you wanted an answer."

"I'm just checking to see if you want to come back to my restaurant, papi."

Her lips puckered, and she sent him a kiss through the air, which was something he appreciated.

"So, what did you do while I was gone?"

"After we spoke, I made my way over to my mom's house, where I spoke with my parents. I told them that my ex, Juan, is fully out of the picture, and that there is someone special in my life now."

"So, you met someone special while I was gone?" he joked.

"No, stupid! I was talking about you! My father has heard of you but wants to meet you face-to-face. My mother has never heard of you, but still wants to meet you, because I told her you were a good man, and she could see that you make me happy."

Deja and Tom's level of chemistry was strong. There was a fast pace of emotions and love developing, even if they did not see it coming themselves.

Tom looked at her as she spoke and felt even more connected to her. She had spoken to her family about him, which he felt was a sign of wanting to be fully committed and serious.

"I guess now I have to face the two people that made you as beautiful as you are?"

"Don't be scared now, papi. You said you wanted me and this relationship."

"I'm not scared. I hope I didn't sound like that, because I was thinking how it was going to be a pleasure to meet them. Plus, I feel lucky to have made it to that level. Most guys don't get to meet the parents."

She smiled and took a sip of her apple martini.

The food arrived and looked just as good as it did on the menu. They both indulged in the freshly prepared sushi.

"This is good, papi. You know all the good

spots to eat!"

"When I get a woman other than my chef to cook for me, I'll eat at home a little more often."

"All you have to do is ask, papi. I can throw down in the kitchen and make all types of Puerto Rican soul food. I call it comfort food."

"No rush, but I look forward to this home-cooked meal with love. For some reason, it tastes better knowing it was cooked with love and a passion for making food."

She loved that he said, "no rush." It showed signs of promise, with more and better days to come, which was something she was looking forward to with him.

"So, how was your business trip, good or no?"

"I bought another property to establish my brand down in Miami. It also gives me an excuse to purchase a home down there to visit whenever I please or reside down there and have my current home as my winter vacation spot."

Tom did not have any kids, which Deja knew just from observation. There were no photos at his place and never any talk of children, but she wondered if he ever wanted them.

"I'm glad for you that things worked out in your favor, so we can enjoy ourselves tonight," she said before she paused and took another bite of her octopus sashimi. "So, did you ever think about having kids?"

"Plural? Not just one at a time?" he said, being funny. "I believe with the right person kids are possible. Marriage is possible, and being a family is too."

"I think we would make beautiful, chocolate Boricua babies," she said, adding humor to the conversation.

"I think making the baby or babies would be

86

the best part because it gives me a chance to make love to you instead of rushing into it. I'll make it special."

"Mmmmmh, it sounds like you know what you're doing. Does this love-making involve being in love?"

She had a way with her words, too, which was always something that Tom noticed. Her words were alluring.

"You could love the person making love to you, or you could love the passion, the intimacy, and the pleasures of love being made to you."

She was feeling like making this love to him right there in the restaurant with sushi flying everywhere, but it was just a thought. Her heart loved how his words massaged it.

"I could see you and me in the near future engaging in such euphoric and pleasant acts; besides, it would give us baby-making practice," she joked, which got Tom to laugh a little harder than normal.

She found this to be a good sign. Her humor and forward mind captivated yet worked on him.

"I like that you can make me laugh just as I can put a smile on your face. It's chemistry at its best!"

"I'm glad you can appreciate my funny side as well as my serious side. It's important to know how to cater to the heart as well as the body. I see good in you, and my heart's instincts tell me you're the one. I never felt this way or thought this way about anyone else."

Tom was feeling her in many ways and also thinking along the same lines as the words she had spoken. It only made him gravitate more toward her mentally and emotionally. He was impressed by how mature she was for her age, and she seemed to know what she wanted out of life.

The conversation continued to develop emotionally between the two of them, which allowed each of them to be pulled into the other's mind and heart as they slowly became one.

As dinner came to an end, all the food and drink were gone. Tom only had two drinks because he was driving. He let Mr. Wilson have the night off, so he drove his snow-white Mercedes Benz AMG CLS with chrome rims, chrome flakes in the paint, custom-stereo system, and custom engine. It was luxury and sport all rolled into one, giving him the best of both worlds. He also looked good with his new better half, Deja.

"You ready to leave, beautiful?"

"I'm ready to snuggle with you in that big

bed, papi."

He helped her to her feet and pulled her close to him, before placing a passionate yet brief kiss onto her warm, glossy lips.

"We can snuggle, baby."

They made their way out of the restaurant after Tom secured the bill and left a generous tip for the server.

Once they were in the car, Tom turned on some slow music to set the mood. R-Kelly's "When a Woman Loves" was playing, which was a song that Tom found growing on him with his new relationship with Deja. She also took to the song, affectionately rubbing his leg as he drove. It only proved to him that she was the woman in the song, because she loved for real.

Chapter 7

om was just waking up at 8:45 a.m. and
starting his day a little later than normal.
Deja was snuggled underneath him just as she
wanted to do last night. This was just as good as
sex, feeling the comfort, compassion, and
closeness of someone special while building on
a future of love and promise.

When Tom moved to get out of the bed, Deja
opened her eyes and wondered where he was
going.

"*Buenos dias*, papi! Where you going?"

"I need to make my way into the office. I may
own Legacy Rentals, but I have to make sure
everything is running smoothly, and everyone is
happy, from my staff to my customers."

"You know I need a job now, since my job was laying people off."

"You already have a job."

"What exactly is that, papi?"

"Looking good and working on being my future wife."

When he said that, her morning started, and her heart, mind, and body were fully awakened.

"I guess I'll be working really hard then to keep you happy?" she said with a smile. "But if you keep being good to me and *mi corazon*, then falling in love with you will be easy."

He came back to the bedside, leaned over, and kissed her lips with morning breath.

"If I didn't like you or feel something strong developing, I would not have kissed that bad breath of yours."

"Your breath stinks too, papi, so don't trip!"

Tom chuckled and then walked into the large

his-and-her bathroom.

She lay back down content with the new man in her life. There was no need to shop around and no need to go backward, meaning engaging with Juan. She was now headed down the path of love.

Tom was in the shower freshening up and getting his thoughts together for the day ahead. He wanted to remain successful, something his father never got a chance to see him do.

Deja walked into the bathroom to brush her teeth before standing outside of Tom's shower.

"Papi, can I wash your back?"

He had his head under the water with his eyes closed in thought when she interrupted his focus time. He was also thinking about something he had seen, the Nike shoebox full of money. He wanted to know why she was carrying it around. He did not want to ask her the previous night because it would have ruined a good night.

"Come on in, baby."

She was excited that he said yes. What man would say no to her in this position?

She grabbed the sponge and the Axe body wash, which she poured on the sponge. She then began to wash his back lovingly. He still was facing the wall with the hot water beating down on his head when he spoke up.

"Baby, what's the story with you carrying that shoebox of money around? You don't trust the banks or something?"

The sponge paused in the middle of his back. She wondered why he asked now when it had been there since last night. He even moved it from the chair to the side of the bed.

"If I tell you, you can't trip, okay, papi?"

Why would I trip! he thought to himself.

"I'm listening, just as long as it's yours."

"It's not my money. It belongs to my ex, Juan Dominguez. You know, the one who went to jail. He got caught with $243,000 cash, plus a gun, but no drugs. That wasn't all of his money. He still had $147,000 that he left at our apartment."

"That doesn't look like $147,000 to me."

"Because it's not. I spent all of it, except for $10,000 that he told me to give to this chick. Now there's $32,000. I didn't think holding it was a problem, papi. I was going to hold it until he got out, which he claims will be soon."

Tom turned around to face her, to make sure he gave her eye contact when he began speaking.

"I appreciate your honesty, but I don't want you to have any connection with your ex, especially when it comes to this money of his."

Tom knew that it was drug money. A person like Juan would not just take $32,000 and walk away as if there was no more to it, especially not coming home to the woman that was once his.

"As for the rest of the cash, you keep it. What I'll do is have my accountant send him a certified check for a $150,000; therefore, he doesn't have a reason to patronize you or this relationship we're in."

Tom viewed paying off the entire sum as insurance, so Juan would not need to think about bringing harm to her. People like that kill for hundreds of dollars, so tens of thousands would not be a second thought.

Her eyes became vitreous from the mixed emotions of happiness and sadness as well as being saved from her debts and emotional ties.

"Thank you, papi," she said, sliding her arms around him and then placing her head on his chest as the hot water beat down on them.

"No secrets, no games, and no lies.

Remember this, and we'll have a good life, and also a future of love," Tom promised before placing a kiss on her forehead. "Now cheer up, baby. Everything is going to be all right as long as you believe in me and our relationship."

Deja handed him the sponge to signify that she wanted her back washed.

"Your turn, papi."

"Like I said before, I don't mind being your love slave."

She giggled as he washed her back with passion. He was gentle and covered every curve of her body while watching the water form beads on top of beads that raced over her flesh and down to her pedicured toes. Tom allowed the soap to wash away while looking on at the art of her beauty. She was so unique and all he ever dreamed of. He wanted to give her the world, both emotionally and financially. Her long wavy hair looked like silk that almost reached the small of her back by a few inches, which added to the picturesque moment.

He placed his lips on her shoulders and dropped the sponge to the shower floor, which freed up his hands to wrap around her. He then caressed her breasts and stimulated the tips by tweaking her in every way. She leaned her head back as his hands dropped lower and slid over her silky landing strip. As he parted her, his finger magic began. She raised her arm up and placed it behind his neck and head. She loved the way his fingers played around her kitty.

"Ahi, ahi, papi! Ahi!"

She loved it, so she spread open her legs to give him all the access he needed.

He rose up fast from behind. She could feel the presence of his love growing on her, and she wanted him to be a part of her in every way.

"Make love to me, papi! Ahi, mmmmh! Make love," she moaned and pleaded, feeling the buildup rushing to its peak.

He stopped the finger magic and allowed her to turn around and face him. Her eyes filled with lust, love, and passion. Her lips found his as she wrapped her arms around his neck and then jumped up.

Tom instinctively caught her while their lips were still connected. She wanted him. She wanted the love emotionally and physically.

He lowered himself to press his fullness against her and then felt her tightness and warmth. She let out a moan as she felt the same pressure against her love spot.

"Aaaaahi, ahi, papi!"

He made his way inside, feeling all of her in every movement. She clenched him hard and loved the way her body felt as he strategically made his moves. As he held her in his grasp, she felt as if she was melting in sensation as the power of passion took over her body.

"Ohhhhh! Mmmmmmmmmmh! Aaaaaaahi, ahi, papi."

She held on tight to his muscular frame as he made love to her slowly hitting her spot over and over and sending an uncontrollable surge of pleasure through her body. Her moans became loud, before the rush of pleasure left her speechless. She locked her lips on his neck, trying to embrace the erupting sensation that was soaring through her. Her teeth came out as she placed love bites on his neck, igniting him and making his slow love-making movement pick up. She was already having multiple orgasms. His fast pace created an overflow of sensation. She clenched all over, from top to bottom, making him explode in passion.

Although he was almost weak in the knees, he maintained control and unleashed his passion inside of her.

He slowed his pace but still felt her letting go. Her lips on his neck stimulated him even more, which allowed him to remain strong.

"You feel so good, baby. I can get used to having this as my good morning and good night," Tom joked but was being truthful.

She giggled as she lifted her lips from his neck and placed a kiss to his lips.

"I felt the passion and emotion of this lovemaking, just as you said I would. I think I could get used to this as well." She kissed his lips once more. "I thought you were going to drop me at the end."

He laughed because he knew what she was talking about.

"And ruin this good thing? Nah, I'm holding

on to all of this."

"Put me down," she requested after placing another kiss to his lips.

She raised back up on her toes and kissed his chest. She nibbled on him like he was real chocolate, and then she began to kiss the rest of his body. He did not resist. She finally picked up the sponge from the shower floor to finish what she had started.

"We can finish when you come home. It will give you something to look forward to. Besides, it's baby-making practice." She laughed.

"I could call in sick," he suggested, which made her laugh. "You're stupid, papi! Like you have someone to answer to!"

"I have you to answer to now. You're the boss of the home front. Well, you will be when baby-making practice pays off."

She loved that he was on the same page as

she was, being humorous while adding a touch of seriousness. Regardless, they were still able to appreciate the conversation of one another.

She finished washing him down, and then he exited the shower to get dressed and head to the office. Once she got out of the shower, she got herself together for the day ahead as well.

She now had the rest of the cash to herself, since Tom was going to pay off Juan. She did not have any plans to spend the cash all at once. She knew it would be best if she got herself a checking or savings account, so she could always have money for a rainy day if needed.

Chapter 8

*M*elanie was taking first lunch at 11:07 a.m., and she was ready to see Juan. Whatever was on the menu did not matter as long as she was able to see him. He was the completion of her day. Melanie was pulled in now, and she gave a part of herself to him. She was emotionally involved, setting her ground and making sure no one got her man. She knew she was the jealous type; however, Juan did not know her little antics she applied when the assumption of a threat came about, whether it be Dawn, Deja, or even her co-worker, Danika, who she ditched eating with that day.

Melanie came through the doors of the staff dining room scanning for Juan, but not being too obvious. She was also checking to see how many people were there, as well as who was there.

Juan noticed her walk through the doors and make her way up to the counter.

"How's everything going today, gentlemen?" she said while making eye contact with Reggie B, Little Man, and Juan.

She was acting different, Reggie B and Little Man thought. She was one of the staff that always looked down on them until Juan started working there.

"How you doing, ma'am?" Reggie asked.

Juan simply nodded his head as he flashed back to the bathroom excitement and wanted an instant replay.

Spaghetti was on the menu, but Melanie was only thinking about dessert: Juan. She wanted him just as she envisioned.

She grabbed her food before she headed to a table.

Juan gave her a few seconds before he made his way over to the table to retrieve her tray, and also to see what was on her mind.

"I thought about you last night," he said with a brief smile.

"Ditto, with a little extra self-entertainment with you in mind," she said with a naughty look.

"Your friend dropped by with the money. She said something about not writing you anymore because she's done with you."

Once again, Melanie was securing all ends and making sure he was not telling her the same thing as he was to her. Juan felt a slight crush to the heart, because he did at one-point love Deja. The moment of heartfelt emotion quickly dissipated, however, when he thought about the remainder of his money.

"What she say about the rest of my money?" he asked, trying not to snap.

Melanie was checking his body language and facial expressions. She wanted to see if he still was connected to her emotionally.

"She didn't really say. Anyway, back to us," she said lowly. "We don't need her. All we need is each other."

When he heard this, he knew she would not be asking for the remainder of the money. Even if she did, he now had a plausible excuse: Deja had abandoned him.

"You're right, *to eres todo lo que necesita en mi vida.*"

Her smile could be seen across the room. She loved how romantic his voice sounded speaking

Spanish to her.

"I don't know what you just said, but it sounded sexy and good to me."

Reggie B and Little Man took notice of the body language and smiles that Melanie kept giving. They knew there was more to her and Juan.

"Young buck, get those trays over there too," Reggie B called, wanting Juan to pick up his pace, since he did not notice the two nurses that sat down and needed their trays collected.

Before he walked away, Melanie got in a quick sentence. She did not want him to leave.

"I got you something."

He made eye contact with her, and she nodded toward the bathroom. He continued to walk away to grab the other trays before he headed back to the counter.

"Good looking, Reggie B. I didn't even see them two come in."

"Ain't nothing, young buck. Just keep your eyes open and play your cards right."

Right then Juan knew that his interaction with Melanie was evident, but Reggie B was smooth. He did not care as long as Juan was low-key and quiet about what he did.

"I got it in line."

Juan stood behind the counter drinking a soda and conversing with Reggie and Little Man as more people entered the dining hall. Juan was thinking about how he was going to make a move with everyone coming in for lunch.

The lunch rush lasted for a few minutes. Although many seats were taken, a lot of the other diners were just about to finish up. When he turned, Melanie was nowhere in sight. Juan knew she had disappeared into the bathroom, but which one?

He grabbed his cleaning supplies before he headed to the bathroom.

He entered the men's room, but there was no Melanie. His heart pounded, and butterflies started to jump around. He knew she was playing around. Although the dining hall was not full, there were plenty of important people around.

He knocked on the women's bathroom door to make sure no one was inside.

No answer. This meant she was in there. His body heated up and his mind raced. He wanted to know what she had for him, and he wanted to know if this was going to be a sex thing. If so, it was okay with him, but risky.

She was in one of the stalls when he entered

the bathroom. He forgot to put up the cleaning sign outside of the bathroom, so no one would enter the bathroom. Melanie stuck her head out from the stall with a smile on her face. She then raised her index finger and gestured for him to come closer.

"Come here, sexy man."

He placed his spray bottle, rags, and toilet brush on the outside of the stall.

She pulled him into the stall and placed passionate kisses to his lips. She was aggressive, which he liked. It was a turn on to him and her. His hands searched her body, and he loved how soft she was.

"What you got for me?" he asked, pulling away from the kiss.

She pulled out a pre-paid Nokia cell phone.

"I want to talk to you right before I go to

sleep, or whenever I'm not here."

He looked into her eyes, seeing how real she was and how emotional she had become so fast.

"Thank you, mami. Don't trip if I wake up at 1:00 in the morning telling you about a dream I had of you."

She laughed and then kissed his lips.

"I won't get mad as long as I'm not having a good dream of you."

"You got the real thing, right here and right now."

She slid down her pants and pulled one leg out, so he could take her love from the front. She raised her leg to allow him to take advantage of her passion. She held on for the ride, closed her eyes, and muffled her moans on his shoulders.

"Mmmmmmh, mmmmmmh! Juan, Juan! Mmmmmmh!" Her mouth opened.

She placed her lips against his ear and breathed heavily. There were no words. She was taken by the intense pleasure escaping from her body.

Her moans and the excitement of the situation all added to his eruption.

His movement became faster and harder. She loved every second of it. Never having this done to her before, she never experienced this level of passion or excitement.

As he filled her with passion, their moment was interrupted when they heard the bathroom door open.

He was still in position as their hearts pounded even harder than before. She clenched him in fear of getting caught and losing the job she just got hired on to. He was in fear of going to the hole and getting transferred, among many other things, such as Melanie saying something else took place, like rape.

His heart pounded so hard that she could feel it as she embraced him.

Melanie pulled away and slid back into her pants as she gestured for Juan to stand on the toilet in case someone looked underneath and saw two sets of legs and feet.

Whoever it was came in just to wash their hands before eating, and then they exited.

They looked at one another as if it was a close call. Juan stepped down onto the floor when the door opened back up. He raised his foot back up on the toilet, thinking to himself that this could not be happening. His heart still was pounding, the heat was rising, his mind still was racing, and he was wondering who it was this time.

"Mr. Dominguez," a female voice spoke

lightly, almost as if she did not want anyone else to hear her call out his name.

Melanie looked at Juan. He still bared the look of a deer in the headlights, because he recognized the voice. It was Dawn. She cleared her throat.

"Juan," she whispered.

Dawn thought he was in there cleaning when she saw his things by the stall, until she bent down and looked under the stall, only to see a set of staff browns and feet. No Juan in sight. Right then she felt embarrassed, hoping that whoever was in the stall did not know who she was talking about.

Melanie heard Dawn call Juan's name. She did not like it either, especially when she caught on to the voice of the person speaking.

When Dawn exited the bathroom, Melanie

looked at Juan and wanted answers.

"Now isn't the time, but why is she calling you like that?"

"Like you said, now isn't the time. I'll call you tonight," he said as he leaned in to kiss her and make her feel all better.

"They want what you got, baby."

She lit up smiling from within. Her heart was all better now. Juan was good, and he knew this about himself, which made him even more emotionally dangerous.

He grabbed his things and slipped out of the bathroom into the men's room. He sprayed the bleach and made it seem like he was working hard. He was also able to cover the sweetness of Melanie's perfume on his body as well as the aroma of passionate sex and body sweat.

When he came back out, Dawn was already

at her table, and Reggie B was grabbing her tray.

He walked over to Juan, and he knew he was obviously up to something.

"Ms. O'Conner asked about you."

"Who?" Juan asked, acting as if he did not know her off hand.

"The redhead over there! She asked where the new guy was, and I told her you were cleaning the bathrooms."

Juan turned around and faced the dining room and saw Dawn smile until Melanie came out of the bathroom area. At that exact moment, her smile vanished just like a magic trick.

There was something about Melanie that Dawn did not 1ike, but she could not put her finger on it. Her woman's instinct allowed her to know she was not right.

Dawn rolled her eyes at Melanie as she

exited the dining hall. Melanie just smirked and gave her a sadistic why-you-calling-my-man look.

Juan made his way over to the table. He wanted to see what was on her mind.

"Can I help you with anything today, counselor?"

"I was looking for you. Your stuff was in the ladies' bathroom."

"I was cleaning the bathroom until I had to go bad," he said while rubbing his stomach, referring to a number two. "I think I ate too much spaghetti."

"Before I leave, I want another kiss."

"That's all you want?" he joked, not really wanting to do that, especially after being with Melanie.

"In due time, when you come home. I want it

to be special, and something we'll cherish, appreciate, and remember because it'll be the first time."

"On a serious note, I got the picture of Breeana. She's a baby doll. Now I understand why you said what you did about the package. I'm not looking to hurt anyone, especially that pretty little girl. How could I explain that?"

His words warmed her from within. He made eye contact with her as he spoke and saw the sparkle in her eyes. She was a hidden treasure waiting to be discovered and cherished.

Dawn was back in the bathroom area about twenty minutes later. Juan's lips were on hers, and his tongue pressed in and out, which ignited emotions and tingling sensations that stirred in their stomachs. The feeling was much better than butterflies. It felt good. Her hands were behind his neck while his hands moved up and down her body. It proved the future of good love flashing before them both as they osculated with fervor. She was happy being in a place of comfort, and each beat of her heart was now for a love she always wanted and yearned for. As for Juan, he wished he was two people, because he really wanted to make both women happy without having to hurt or leave the other. Besides, Melanie was the key to his release. If he made her mad, she could change this. If he made Dawn mad, she would venture off and check up behind Melanie's computer artifice.

Chapter 9

Juan was in his cell at 3:45 p.m. checking out the apps on his new cell phone that Melanie slid to him in the bathroom. He did not want to call her right away. He figured he would give her until 5:00 p.m. to settle in after working until 4:00 p.m.

As he fondled the phone, Puto looked out for him and stood on the cell gate.

"*Oye*, Juan, *agua* coming with the mail," Puto said.

"*Bien, me tengo eso,*" he responded after tucking the phone and acting like he was watching TV.

The guard stopped at his cell.

"Sanchez, one for you. Dominguez, three for

you."

Puto grabbed the letters and handed them to Juan.

"Who wrote you, Puto?"

"*Mi novia de* Mexico."

"Okay, that's a good look for you right there. Now you have somebody in your corner."

"*Yo no se.* She probably wants *mi chabo.*"

They laughed together, knowing how it was when it came to women wanting money to do whatever it is they did. Sometimes they never had anything to show for it other than clothing and jewelry.

Juan left Puto to read his mail while he focused on Deja's letter. He wanted to know what she wrote, especially after hearing what Melanie said about her earlier.

He opened the letter and noticed the smeared ink from her tears that saturated the paper as she wrote it out. A necessary cry she needed to release before beginning with her new life and new love.

Dear Juan:

I can't do this anymore with you. I admit, I messed us up running off with your money, and you ruined us by going to jail. It doesn't make us even; it just makes this the end of our relationship and puppy love. You're right, money can be spent, and love can be wasted. I'm going to spend my time finding true love. Tom's his name, and he's the one who bought the bracelet. He's the one my heart now belongs to, and the one that feels so right. If you love me as you say you do, then love me enough to let me go. But know that I love you as a friend for showing me the way up until this point. Take care. I wish for you to be safe in there and get out soon. Your money will be okay, so don't trip.

Bye-bye,

Deja

A part of his heart was crushed reading this,

and a slight knot formed in his throat. The emotions he was feeling were mixed. He was thinking about all they went through, but then she bounced after spending almost all his money. He wanted his money. She was not going to play him out like that. He turned to tell Puto what was going on but was cut short when the officer came over the intercom in the cell.

"Dominguez, report to the counselor's office."

The door buzzed open. His mind raced again because he wanted to know who it was. It could not be Dawn, because she should have been heading home by this time.

When he came out of his cell, he saw the unit manager alone with the security captain standing by the counselor's office.

The first thing that came to his mind was that he was compromised. Someone had told them about Melanie or Dawn.

He walked up with a confused look on his face.

"Dominguez, step in the office."

The captain led the way with a few papers in his hand and an envelope. After seeing the documents, Juan was certain that they were onto his sentence.

They all took a seat except for the captain, who remained standing to show his superiority.

"We have a situation, Mr. Dominguez," the unit manager said as he reached for the papers from the captain.

Situation? Damn, they're onto me! Juan thought.

"A large sum of money was mailed to you today via certified check from the Jones Corporation."

What the hell is the Jones Corporation? Juan

thought.

"Why do you need so much money here when you're due to leave in less than five months now?"

The unit manager knew Juan got caught with a large sum of money, so this was not looking good.

"Jones Corporation you said, right?" Juan asked again, trying to get more information.

"Tom Jones with Legacy Rentals, Warren Charles restaurants, real estate."

Hearing this information clicked in Juan's mind as to who he was, since Deja had mentioned his name in the letter. Juan wanted to know the amount.

"How much money did Tom send?" Juan asked as if he knew it was coming by mentioning him on a first-name basis as if he really knew him.

"It was for $150,000," the security captain blurted out while searching for Juan's reaction.

The captain hated that this amount was three years' pay for him, and that a drug dealer was still getting large sums of money.

"So, what exactly is the problem?"

"For security reasons, an inmate is only allotted a maximum of $10,000 here at the CDCC. The rest can be forwarded to an account."

Juan felt a load off, now knowing that he had his money back. He knew Tom paid this off for Deja's mishap, and he also understood the reason behind it. Deja still did not know when Juan was coming home, which was a plus for him, especially having his money back.

"Well, if the Inmate Account Department can set me up an account with Commerce Bank, it would be appreciated. Send the entire check to them. I have enough on my account right now."

The captain looked at Juan because he knew he already had enough. In fact, he was sitting on a few thousand on his books, which was more than the captain had in his own checking account.

"We'll need your signature, and then you can head back to your cell," the unit manager said.

Juan signed the paper before exiting the office. The block sergeant and officers looked on at him as he strolled to his cell. Knowing that he just had received all this money put envy all over their faces. Juan loved every second of it as he turned and saw them looking at him before he stepped into his cell.

He was back where he needed to be. He would head home back on top-10 brick money, or 5 and go-on-vacation money.

He shared the good news with Puto, but he

did not seem too excited.

"*Que pasol*, bro? You looking like the letter you got was bad news."

"*Mi novia, dice to habla con policia.* FBI."

Juan was shocked to hear this, because he was not a snitch. In fact, he hated snitches.

"I don't even like them cabrons! What you talking about?"

Puto's girlfriend was contacted by Donna Tulia's people. She knew that Juan and Puto were in the same prison. Information they found out via the DOC's JNET website allowed the public to learn where inmates were located and how much time they had remaining.

The cartel was checking up on all its associates and those recently incarcerated. They were trying to find the mole, and they were unaware that the mole was a deep undercover FBI agent infiltrating the organization. The cartel felt that Juan was the problem since his sentence went from eight and a half to seventeen years and then down to one to two years within weeks after being sentenced. This sent red flags all over the board. So, they knew that Juan had paid for this adjustment.

"You cut the time. How did you do that?"

Juan never told Puto what he was doing or how he was doing it. He did not want to jinx himself or have anyone tell on him.

He broke it down to Puto from the letters to Dawn and Melanie. He even showed Puto the content of the letter, so he would know that he was telling the truth.

Puto was born in Mexico and worked for the cartel, so he knew that death came to all those who crossed the cartel. He needed to get word to them, since he felt that Juan was telling the truth.

Donna Tulia sent the order for Puto to carry out the hit. In return, he would be rewarded upon release.

Puto became all right with Juan. He could not just take him out without asking questions, which was a good thing because Juan would be dead right now.

"Don't worry, amigo, I'll take care of this," Puto said after shaking Juan's hand to assure him that he was a man of his word.

Juan sat back down at the desk and finished reading Melanie's and Dawn's letters. He could not focus like he wanted to, because he was thinking about the cartel, the money that Tom Jones had sent, and Deja. A lot of bad was happening that outweighed the good. To top it off, he now needed to watch his back. He could not trust Puto or the cartel's decision to take him out at any given time.

Chapter 10

*M*elanie walked into the staff dining hall at 11:01 a.m. showing her emotions clearly on her face. She was upset that Juan did not call her last night, and she wanted to know why.

She walked up to the counter, grabbed her food, and headed to her table without speaking to Juan, only to Reggie B and Little Man. Juan did not like this. Now she was acting up, he thought.

He made his way over to her table to retrieve her tray.

"What's your face broke up for?"

"You didn't call me last night. You needed to explain why that bitch was calling you in the bathroom."

Right then he saw how emotionally involved she had become, as well as how possessive she was.

"So much went on last night. But the good thing about yesterday is that I got all my money back."

When he said that, she thought about the amount he was arrested with.

"The bad thing is that people think I'm a snitch because of this sentence change. That's what I was taking care of last night. I can't have people thinking that about me. It's not a good look."

"Can you make sure you call me today?" she asked, not caring about the other stuff he was talking about.

She sent her words with a smile, but she still wanted to get to the bottom of why Dawn was calling him in the bathroom.

"As soon as you leave, I'll call you. Let's say around 4:00 p.m."

Juan stopped speaking in mid-speech and walked away when he saw Sergeant Stern step through the door.

"Dominguez! What up, playa?" His tone was a little different than normal as he approached Juan. "I hear you're sitting heavy on the cash. Hood-rich, huh?" He gave Juan an eye trying to figure him out.

"You know my boy Tom Jones? I went to school with him."

"Not really, but we have a mutual associate."

Sergeant Stern put his arm around Juan and pulled him close and firm as he spoke low. "You need anything, just let me know. Just spread the financial love, playa."

He was talking about Juan's money. He was

willing to bring a package in if he wanted it, or a phone—the usual contraband.

Juan did not say anything. He just nodded his head as the sergeant walked away.

Melanie wanted to speak with him, because she was not finished talking to him. She could not head to the bathroom because of the sergeant being there. It was bothering her she could not have her way; and to make matters worse, Dawn walked into the dining hall. Now Juan was faced with dealing with both of the ladies. At first glance, it looked as if they planned it; but on Dawn's behalf, it was her woman's instinct to want to check up on the man who was supposed to be hers.

Melanie checked out Dawn's facial expressions and body language. At the same time, she kept an eye on Juan to make sure he did not send any passes Dawn's way.

Dawn sent a smile his way, and he acknowledged it and smiled back. He was just lucky that Melanie missed it because she was caught in the middle of turning her head.

Juan thought about how close this was. In fact, it was too close for comfort, especially if Sergeant Stern left. He figured that one of the women would ask him to go to the bathroom, which was something he was not looking forward to today.

Juan checked the time because he knew that Melanie's lunch break was almost over. But time seemed to move very slowly—too slow for him.

Melanie wanted to put her foot down and make sure there was nothing between the two of them. Sergeant Stern was exiting when she made a pass to Juan to head to the bathroom. He acted as if he did not see her, which only made her even more upset.

Melanie got up and made her way toward the counter. Upon seeing her head his way, his heart started to pound. He could not believe what she was doing, or thought she was getting ready to do.

"Mr. Dominguez, can I get the spray bottle to clean off the seat in the restroom? It's kind of crazy in there."

"Young buck, that should be cleaned up in there," Reggie B said, not knowing what Melanie was doing.

Juan quickly turned to him so he could see his facial expression.

"I'll clean that for you, ma'am," Reggie B said, taking one for the team.

"Then again, I'll just use the bathroom in reception. I have to hurry back over there and make some adjustments to these files."

Juan did not like that one bit. It was actually

a turn-off in a major way. He needed to figure out something quick. He could not afford a change back to the eight and a half to seventeen years of incarceration.

"You don't have to rush over there. I'll personally clean this off for you."

Juan headed into the bathroom with his spray bottle. Dawn watched him disappear into the bathroom. As Melanie followed behind him, Dawn stood up. She was not going to sit and allow this to happen.

"Don't ever threaten me like that!" Juan said before he pulled her in close for a kiss. She let it happen because she was having her way. "I'll call you today, I promise. Just don't do this again!"

She smirked. She loved that he was under her control, just when he thought he was controlling her.

"You want me? I have a few more minutes

until my break's over?"

He kissed her once more to make her happy.

"No, maybe tomorrow!"

Just as those words came out of his mouth, the bathroom door opened. Juan was quick to slide into the stall and begin to spray it down. Melanie turned to the sink and began to wash her hands. At the same time, she looked into the mirror and saw Dawn standing next to her.

They did not speak, but they were thinking the same thing. Neither of them wanted each other to have Juan. Yet neither of them knew how far Juan was into both of them emotionally, mentally, and as for Melanie, physically.

Dawn quickly scanned the bathroom and saw Juan in the stall.

"Are you almost done in here? I need to use the bathroom."

"I'm sorry, ma'am. I'm just finishing up," he

replied while wiping off the toilet before exiting the bathroom and leaving the two women to themselves.

Melanie rolled her eyes as she exited the bathroom. Dawn smacked her teeth, but a part of her wanted answers. She wanted to know what Juan was doing with her, if anything at all. She also wondered to herself what she had gotten herself into with him.

~ ~ ~

At 1:24 p.m., Deja and Tom were just coming out of the home theater after watching *Man on Fire* starring Denzel Washington. It was one of many movies in which they shared a common interest.

The doorbell rang and chimed through the large estate. Tom was expecting guests. He checked his watch to see what time it was. Anita was in the kitchen preparing a late lunch for them and their guests. Brandi answered the door and allowed the guests inside. Tom came up to the main level in the elevator.

Deja held his hand as they walked out of the elevator into the foyer, where she heard people speaking her language—people whose voices she recognized. When she walked into the foyer, she saw that it was her mother and father.

She looked at Tom and could not believe how thoughtful he was. She raised up on her toes and kissed him passionately.

"Thank you, papi!"

"You said I should meet your parents. I felt a need to bring them here, so they know that their daughter is in good hands."

Deja's parents were taken aback when they saw the large, sumptuous home. It was something they only saw on television. Deja walked over to them and gave them both big hugs out of love.

"Mami! Papi! This is Tom Jones. Tom, this is Mr. and Mrs. Rodriguez."

"*Llamame* Carlito, Tom," Deja's father said.

"Nice to meet you, Carlito, and Mrs. Rodriguez."

"You live nice, Señor Jones. *Mi hija* means the world to me, so make sure you take good care of her no matter what," Carmen said, being a mother. "Because all of this is good, but love is better," she added.

"I know, and one day your daughter and I will have that love that will be richer than anything in the world."

Deja loved his words, and she knew that he meant them.

"*Yo te lo dije,* mami. He's a good man, after *mi corazon.*"

"Deja, give your mother a tour of the house

while I speak to your father over a cold beer."

"Beer sounds good. He's a keeper, nena," Carlito joked as he followed Tom into the kitchen.

"Smells good in here!" Carlito said after seeing the chef working her kitchen magic.

"Carlito, this is my wonderful chef, Anita. Anita, this is Deja's father, Carlito."

"Nice to meet you, sir," she said with a smile. "The food will be ready in a few minutes. Where would you like it to be set up?"

"Outside under the pavilion," Tom responded.

He grabbed two Corona beers out of the refrigerator and handed one to Carlito.

"Let's talk about why you're here, sir," Tom said, making his way out to the family room.

They took a seat on the plush leather seats across from one another.

"*Mi hija* seems happy with you. You do good for her, she says. Better than the last guy. He didn't work, but had plenty of money, you know what I mean?" Tom knew, since he paid Juan his money, so he could not patronize their relationship. "You, Tom, I see a real thing between you and mi hija. The same thing I saw in myself when I was first dating Carmen." He took a few gulps of his beer before finishing. "Always be good to mi hija. She deserves you, and you deserve her."

"Thank you, Mr. Rodriguez. Coming from you, sir, it is an honor and a privilege. So, when the time comes, I have your permission to make her my wife?"

Carlito chugged the rest of his beer before he looked back at Tom.

"You have my permission."

Tom was happy inside. This was feeling real

to him.

Their conversation was cut short when they heard Deja and Carmen laughing and talking as they stepped into the family room.

"This is the family room, Ma. The two sexy men come with it. One for you and one for me," Deja said as she walked over to Tom and placed a kiss on his cheek and then his lips.

"Are you two being nice to one another in here?" Deja asked.

"We have beer, nena," Carlito said. "It's always nice with beer. Besides, I think he loves you."

Carlito knew Tom was falling for his daughter. It was a rare thing to find a love like this, but it was the real thing. Carmen knew this, just as Carlito did.

Deja's heart embraced the words her father just had said. She knew that he knew something she wanted to know and something she wanted to hear from Tom to make her all the way complete.

Tom did not deny what he was saying, which made her heart open up to him even more. She, too, felt a strong and irresistible emotion of love coming on.

She leaned in and wrapped her arms around Tom from behind. She kissed his neck and then his cheek.

"I feel the same about you," she whispered into his ear, making the embarrassment come with ease, since her father put him out there.

"Never hide your true emotions with the one you want to be with, son," Carlito said. "Say what you feel, mean what you say, and do as you say always. The rest will come to you as a reward."

Tom took in Carlito's words, knowing they

were all too true.

Anita walked into the room with Brandi.

"Lunch is set up under the pavilion as requested. If you need anything else, let me know," Anita said.

"Another beer would be nice, por favor," Carlito said.

"Beer is already set up out there in the buckets of ice."

"I may not want to leave here, Tom, if her food is as good as the service," Carlito laughed.

They all made their way outside to the pavilion where the lunch spread looked just as good as it smelled.

Deja was happy that both of her parents really liked Tom and got along well with him.

The food was devoured, and beers were chugged by Tom and Carlito. Deja and her mother drank piña coladas.

Deja was happy inside and out. Both of her parents noticed, which made them glad for her.

This was just the beginning of her happiness. Tom knew how to treat her. He knew what to say and when to say it. He did not want to lose this good thing; that was Juan's mistake.

Chapter 11

*T*wo and a half months passed by, and Juan was now in the best position with Dawn and Melanie. Both women said they loved him. Dawn fell into this love the hardest. She felt strongly about this man being the one for her. Letters flowed in daily, and they could not get enough of each other. They even arranged for daily kisses in the bathroom. Dawn wanted more, but she wanted making love to him to be special. She wanted him to take his time loving her, just as she dreamed and fantasized about.

Breeana was also introduced to Juan via letter and photos. She was told that he was working at the prison rather than being there as an inmate. It was something Dawn felt a need to keep away from her, since she told her daughter all the guys she worked around were bad people. That is why they were in there.

Melanie also took full advantage of falling in love with Juan. She had the opportunity to have him whenever she wanted during the weekday, which added to the excitement of their relationship. It provided her with an emotional and sexual rush, that was not just intriguing but gravitating.

~ ~ ~

Dawn was at home sleeping at 6:59 a.m. There was just one minute until her alarm was set to go off and wake her before she started her day, which was something to which she looked forward. She was in one of her deep dream states filled with thoughts of Juan, their family, and their love. Being pregnant with his child added to the love they already had, and it made them form an even stronger bond.

However, her dream came to an end at the buzzing of the alarm clock next to her head. Her eyes opened, and a part of her did not want the dream to end because it felt so good. But another part of her was ready to start the day, knowing she would see the man she loved and the man with whom she would spend her future. Besides, waking up meant she was another day closer to being with him in the flesh when he came home.

Juan made Dawn aware of the amount of money he had received. She knew about talk of an inmate receiving a large sum of money, but it did not move her as much as it did the others. However, she knew it would give the relation-ship stability. She and Juan talked about investing the money into a business that would have less overhead and a higher return.

She slid out of the bed and made her way to Bree's room to wake her up, so she could get ready for school. She then headed into the bathroom to freshen up for the day ahead. Within thirty minutes they were both ready as they headed out of the house on their way to school and then work.

While Dawn made her way to drop off Breeana in New Cumberland, Melanie was bent over the toilet seat throwing up. Morning sickness was taking her over. At first she did not know what was going on, until she started placing all of the pieces together, missing her monthly period, and now this.

The thought of being pregnant made her even happier, and she knew that she and Juan would make beautiful babies. She believed it was something that Deja or Dawn were not the first to do, or would ever get a chance to do, since she was locking him down with her emotionally, mentally, and physically.

Melanie held her hair back with one hand while her other hand held onto the porcelain seat. A few minutes passed before she was finished tossing up. She immediately stood up and brushed her teeth to rid the taste in her mouth. As she brushed her teeth, she stared in the mirror at herself and thought about becoming a mom, along with the responsibility, the love with Juan, and the future of being a family.

She was also aware of the money. In fact, Juan managed to give her more money until she started falling in love with him. At that point, the money became moot. Her emotions and being with him were much more important.

She rinsed out her mouth, washed her face, and then rubbed her belly with a big grin on her face.

"Is somebody in there?" she asked lovingly. "If you are, Mommy is going to take good care of you."

Melanie knew if she was pregnant that she could not tell her co-workers who the lucky guy was, because it would get her into trouble legally and she would get fired. Juan would also get transferred and have his sentence extended. She did not want to risk this, so she would have to come up with something when she started to show.

Once she got dressed, she headed to work and made a stop at the Rite Aid to pick up a pregnancy test.

As soon as she arrived at work, she entered the bathroom and opened up the pregnancy test. She urinated on it and received a quick response within minutes. At first glance, her heartbeat picked up and butterflies filled her stomach. She witnessed a plus sign, which meant that she was indeed pregnant. The reality of being a mother was setting in. She took another test just in case; and within minutes, the same result appeared.

She took a seat on the toilet. She then closed her eyes and embraced the moment as tears of happiness streamed down the side of her face. She rubbed her stomach, knowing she was now carrying a precious gift from God inside of her. It was certainly a blessing and a part of Juan. The thought of all this made her heart beat for Juan's love even more.

Visions of their future became vivid and real to her. She could not wait until her lunch break to see him.

Melanie pulled herself together and wiped away her tears of happiness. She glowed from the inside and out as she was ready to start her day.

As she left the bathroom, Dawn passed by her, rolling her eyes at her as usual. Ever since she came into the bathroom months before, she knew something was up. She just could not come to ask Juan what he was doing, just in case he was not doing anything other than his job.

Melanie responded to Dawn's rolling eyes with a smirk. She knew she had something she wanted, which was Juan, and now a baby inside of her.

~ ~ ~

It was 10:59 a.m. and Melanie was taking her lunch a minute early. She yearned to see Juan and was very anxious to share the good news with him.

When she entered the dining hall, Reggie B tapped Juan's arm now knowing that was his little thing, but not knowing that they were freaking in the bathroom.

Juan raised his head to see her enter with a smile from ear to ear and glowing radiantly.

He was feeling the love for her. She had something about her that made him appreciate the person she was. Even with her strong jealous side, it was just her wanting his undivided attention, which was something she did not get in her last relationship.

Melanie walked up to the counter to speak with all three men.

"Good morning, gentlemen. I hope your day is going as good as mine."

Juan knew that she was up to something. Now he could not wait to see what it was.

She took a tray and headed over to the salad bar. She made herself a healthy salad and grabbed an apple and an orange. She bypassed the soda fountain that day, and then made her way to a table in the corner.

Juan came behind her seconds later. When he grabbed her tray, he noticed her light, healthy lunch.

"Good morning, baby," Melanie said with her eyes lit up with a different sparkle, making him feel good about seeing her. It was the unique connection they shared.

"It would be a good morning if I knew why my girl is as happy as you are, and why you changed your diet all of a sudden."

She stuck the fork into the freshly made salad, took a bite and then another, wiped the corner of her mouth, and broke into a smile.

"We're pregnant," she said in a low tone with food still in her mouth.

He heard what she said, and it made his heartbeat pick up.

"I didn't hear you. Your mouth was full."

She cleared her mouth, chasing the remaining food down with the lemonade.

"I'm pregnant. I mean, we're pregnant!"

A part of him celebrated inside about having a baby for the first time. But the other half of him realized what this meant. The love he had established with Dawn was going to change, or was it? Did he have what it took to be a man to one of the women? He struggled with this because he wanted both of them to be happy, and he wanted both of them to have love and be loved.

"Bathroom!" he said as he walked away to get his cleaning supplies.

She gave him a chance to leave her table before she made her way to the bathroom. He then walked in a minute later.

After they were inside the bathroom, he held her with affection. He then placed kisses on her and displayed how much he cared for her as he rubbed her stomach.

"So, we're going to have a baby boy, huh?"

"What makes you think it's going to be a boy?" she questioned in her loving tone.

"That's what I want!" he said as he kissed her soft lips. "I gave you what you wanted. Now let's hope I get what I want."

She gazed into his eyes and saw so much promise now. This love was finally happening to her. Something and someone good had come into her life.

"I have to tell my parents, but I'm going to wait until you come home, so I don't have to explain where you are."

"I understand. I guess we're going to have to spoil my junior, so I'm going to write the bank and have them send you some money. I'll also set up an account for our son, so he'll have something to fall back on when he gets older."

So much was running through her mind that she was becoming emotional. She wanted him to come home right now. She did not want to let go of his warm embrace. She was in her comfort zone with him.

"I'm going to be a good mother, Juan. I just

want you to know that."

"I know you are. You have all of the qualities and morals to do so. Besides, I'll be there to keep you in line, and you can wake up and feed the baby in the middle of the night." He laughed.

"Don't worry about that, because I want to breastfeed. I've heard so much good about women doing that."

They were having a loving moment and celebrating the good news, so they did not realize the time.

"Young buck!" Reggie B yelled out for Juan.

"Call me tonight, baby, so we can have some baby talk," she said before slipping out of the bathroom.

Juan followed seconds later with his cleaning supplies.

"What up, Reggie B?"

"I was holding you down while you cleaned the bathroom. I was making sure you was on point."

"I'm good. Everything is cool in there. I need to hit the countertops and fill the toilet paper up," Juan responded with a quick lie.

Juan stood behind the counter and watched Melanie exit. She was now the mother of his child, and he was flying high. He felt good, and love was running through his body.

Dawn walked by and changed his demeanor and smile. He needed to stay focused, so Dawn could stay happy too. Dawn walked up to the counter, grabbed her food, and said hello before she headed back to her table.

Juan walked over to her and saw that she, too, was glowing, but her glow was that of love, the love she felt in her heart for him.

"Hey, baby, I'm counting down the days until you come home. I can't wait to spend my life with you," she said, with love in her sparkling eyes.

"I'm looking forward to that day because it's a day I'm going to celebrate you and our love," he responded so casually, as if she was the only one.

His words meant more now. She loved him, so anything he said stimulated her heart, mind, and body.

She shined with a smile on her face and in her eyes as he walked away. He did not want to stay at the table too long. Besides, in a few minutes, he was going to get his private time with her.

A few minutes passed by before Dawn was standing with her back against the wall, just as she did the first time she shared a passionate kiss with him. The butterflies stirred in her stomach just as they did the first time as well. Her heart loved this feeling, just as much as she loved falling in love with Juan.

He turned the corner, and she opened her arms wanting him. He pulled her close, and their lips melted passionately that very instant. Melanie was no longer a thought. It was Dawn's time, and her kiss meant so much to him each time they shared this unique moment.

She pulled away yet stayed in control. She felt her body heat up with a tingling sensation as if she was ready to erupt.

"I love you, Juan," she said, panting sexually and wanting him right there. "Touch me, baby," she requested, being a little edgy that morning.

It caught Juan by surprise; however, he

obliged. He placed his lips back on hers as his left hand slid down to her love spot and pressed against her dress. A light moan came out, which was something she could not control.

"Oooh, mmmmh."

He continued moving his hand up and down and around on her, before he stopped and opened up the women's bathroom. She followed behind him. They made their way into the stall. He slid her dress up, pulled her panties to the side, and stroked her with his fingers.

"Aaaah, mmmmmh! I like this," she said feeling good.

She wanted to resist while thinking about her job and thinking about how she wanted it to be so perfect—just the way it was in her dreams and fantasy. But his finger magic took her under control. Then he got down and came face-to-face with her pretty, silky red hair, which matched the top. It was cut in a triangle shape that pointed in the right direction.

He placed his lips on her and kissed her love, before taking his tongue on an erotic tour. She grabbed his head and held him in position while trying to muffle her moans.

"Mmmmmmmh, mmmmmmmh! Oh God!"

His fast fingers assisted in the magic show and made her feel the sensation soar through her body. It was coming. She could not resist or stop him—or the eruption—if she tried. Her moans climaxed as well, but they were not loud enough to be heard outside the bathroom.

She was at the point of no return and was flowing out full of pleasure the more Juan's fingers stroked her love and assisted his tongue talk with the kitty. Her legs tensed up, and she had uncontrollable releases. Juan literally had her at his fingertips. The cycle of release came to a halt, only because Juan stopped. He then wiped her down with one of his clean towels and then his face.

A tear slid down her face. The multiple orgasms made her emotions open up even more. She did not want to lose him, and she did not want anyone else to have this man, this love, and this good oral that she had in him.

"Why you crying, beautiful?" he asked as he pulled her in close to comfort her.

"I'm okay. They're good tears. Just make sure you love me the way you say you love me."

"I love you, Dawn. This in itself should be enough for you to know that my heart is with you. I'm coming home to you and your love, and that good tasting love right there," he said, bringing a smile to her face. "Now, let's get out of here before someone walks in on us."

When he said that, she flashed back to when she walked in and saw him with Melanie in the bathroom. But that thought was discharged when he lovingly caressed her back.

"I love you for real, Dawn. You mean so much to me. Next time we become intimate, I want it to be at home, so it can mean something to both of us. I want to make love to you," he said, knowing it would be better when he took his time.

She previously thought the same, but she could not resist what was going on. She did not say a word. Her heart loved that he said this, her body loved what he just did, and her mind was set on loving him forever.

Chapter 12

*T*om and Deja pulled up to the Baltimore Renaissance Hotel & Resort on Pratt Street at the Inner Harbor where they had reservations at Windows Restaurant for 7:45 p.m. Tom also had his assistant, Brandi, make reservations for the presidential suite that overlooked the harbor, with its views of the skyline, landmarks, and yachts on the water.

Their relationship was growing more and more each day. Deja loved him, and he loved her.

The Rolls Royce Phantom came to a halt as Mr. Wilson got out and opened Tom's door. He stepped out wearing a black dinner suit, platinum cufflinks, and a Breitling watch. Deja followed and looked Hollywood fabulous and celebrity elite. She wore a red Versace dress, black Vera Wang stilettos, diamond hoops, and the diamond bracelet that Tom had bought her. She complemented Tom as he did her.

They made their way up to the restaurant on the fifth floor and were seated with a view of the Harbor. Candlelight set the romantic evening.

"They have some of the best seafood here, as you may already know," Tom said.

"You look good tonight, babe," Deja said, looking on at her man with love. "I think we can skip dinner and go to dessert, with you being my chocolate sundae," she joked.

"I love that you know how to make me laugh. Trust me, tonight is going to be special. We can have each other for dessert."

"I hope it's going to be special."

The server came over and handed them menus.

"Welcome to Windows at the Harbor. My name is Manuel, and I'll be catering to your needs this evening. Can I start you off with a drink?"

"I'll have a Long Island ice tea, and she'll have an apple martini."

"Babe, I don't want to drink tonight. Manuel, *dame un batido de fresas, por favor.*"

"I'll go get the drinks while you two check out the menu."

When Manuel walked away, Tom gave Deja a look and searched her face. He wondered why she did not want a drink.

"Is everything okay, babe?"

"I'm okay."

"Why are you not drinking?"

She smiled looking into his eyes with love.

"I'm pregnant, papi. I found out today. I'm a couple months now!"

"I came here to show you a good time, but this is better than anything else. I can't wait to be a dad and have a family with you."

He stood up from his seat and walked around to give her a passionate kiss.

"We're going to give our baby the world. You know if we have a little girl, I'm going to spoil her, so don't get jealous," he said, which made her giggle.

"Stop being crazy! I won't get jealous. If we have a baby girl, she'll be our little princess."

Manuel came back with the drinks.

Tom sat back on the other side across from Deja. He appreciated the view of her even more now. As a mother-to-be, she looked good to him.

"Gracias, Manuel," Tom said, using what little Spanish he learned from Deja. "Tonight, I want you to tell the chef to surprise us with what he's feeling."

"No problema, señor!"

Tom also had good news, and he was ready to reveal something special to Deja. Finding out she was pregnant made his next move all worth it.

The food arrived, and conversation followed. Deja was clearly eating for two now. For dessert, Deja ordered the caramel apple cheesecake while Tom had the chef's gourmet chocolate cake with strips of vanilla ice cream.

"Oh, papi. This cheesecake is so good!" she said while taking her knife and cutting a piece for him. He thought about their first date when she did the same thing with her food.

"This is good. I like that you share, instead of eating the pie and then telling me about it," he said, which made her laugh.

Tom then slid out of his seat. He reached into his pocket to pull out a flawless, four-carat diamond set in white gold with diamond cuts around the band. Her eyes lit up, and her heart fluttered with love. The future flashed before her, and her eyes became vitreous. She was happy and complete.

"Deja, I always tell you how much I care about you. I even show you in many ways, but there are so many ways to show you that I care. I love you, and I mean this from the bottom of my heart. I never felt the way I do right now as I do for you. I want to keep feeling this way with you for the rest of my life, if you take this ring and accept this proposal to be my wife."

This was the first time he said he loved her. She knew in her heart and mind that this was true love. His words were real. She extended her left hand.

"Yes, yes, yes! I'll marry you any day. I love you, too, and now we can be a family with our baby."

He slid the ring onto her finger, feeling the love enhancing by the second.

"Stand up, papi, so I can kiss and hug you."

He stood up and took her in his embrace. He felt her soft, warm lips along with the love and passion in the kiss.

She paused from the kiss and looked up into his eyes.

"I'm glad I have you in my life, and I cherish every day with you. I don't want this ever to end. I feel the love through my heart, mind, and body whenever I'm with you."

Her words touched his heart and allowed him to know that he made the right decision to make her his wife.

"You know now that you're not just the sexiest mom-to-be, but you're the sexiest wife-to-be as well," he said, before placing another kiss on her glossy lips.

"I can't wait to tell my mom and show her and my dad the ring."

"I think they'll agree that I made a good decision, especially when they find out we're having a baby."

"I can wait and call her in the morning, but right now, I think we should head up to the suite where we can have a little celebration of our own. First the baby and now the engagement! I think you deserve a good treat, papi," Deja said, placing another loving kiss to his lips.

"This is going to be the best night thus far. I'm looking forward to this treat as well as giving you a treat of my own—a treat of making love to you, with you knowing how much I love you."

She could feel the love race through her body as she held on to him. This day would always be remembered, and their love would always last as long as they loved each other the same.

They made their way up to the lavish suite with a priceless view of the harbor that surpassed the resort's motto: "The only thing better than the food is the view."

Tom carefully removed her dress to expose her bare body. She had on no panties and no bra. She was the secret, so there was no need for Victoria's underwear. He kissed down her body, stopping at her belly, where he placed kisses and rubbed her stomach with his hand.

"Hey, you, inside there, Daddy is going to take good care of you and Mommy forever."

She thought it was so cute how he talked to her belly and their unborn child.

He continued on with his kisses, kissing her love spot and then making his way back up. She assisted him out of his clothing. Their warm flesh embraced. He then picked her up and carried her over to the tinted, floor-to-ceiling window. But they could still see the lights of the harbor, the passing cars below, and the stars in the sky.

She wrapped her legs around him and held on until they made it to the window. He let her down and placed kisses to her lips, neck, and breasts before turning her around to face the picturesque view. His hands wrapped around her and cupped her breasts as he placed his mouth on her neck, which was the spot that turned her on the most. He placed himself inside her from behind. Her moans filled the room with love and passion.

"Ahi, ahi! I love you, papi!"

"I love you too," he said while continuing to make love to her mind, heart, and body.

Her hands raised up against the window to embrace all of him. Her panting and moans fogged the window by her face. Love was being made, which was something they both enjoyed and appreciated. It made their new engagement more special and made this love unique.

Chapter 13

It was 1:36 p.m. on Thursday, August 4, 2011, the day before Juan was to be released after spending a year incarcerated. He made his rounds and signed out to be released. It was the day that Melanie had looked so forward to, especially now that she was a full five months pregnant and looking sexier by the day.

Melanie took off on Friday. She knew that Juan was coming home, so she planned so much with him. Their love was elevated to the next level. The baby coming assisted in his emotions toward her. Juan spoiled Melanie with his love and money. He wanted to make her the happiest mother-to-be.

Juan also loved Dawn in many ways, and he

made her fall deeply in love with him. She, too, took off the following day. She had planned the entire weekend and first night all for him, their love, and their relationship.

As he made his rounds, Dawn came across the walkway. He saw her approaching with a smile. He could not resist smiling back when he saw her. She was glowing with love and happiness. She knew that her world was about to change. She would now have Juan's love in her life, and they would no longer have to sneak around, even though that part of the relationship was exciting.

"Good afternoon, Mr. Dominguez," she said, a few feet away from him.

"How are you feeling today, Ms. O'Conner?"

"I'll be better tomorrow and even happier once we get married. I got the ring yesterday."

Juan paid Sergeant Stern to buy a two-carat

diamond ring for Dawn. He also paid extra for him to stay hushed about their relationship. Stern knew Juan was smooth, but he did not see that coming or the $5,000 he got to be quiet.

Juan's heart was into Dawn. She was wife material, just as he thought when he first met her. She was a keeper. The ring made her feel loved and appreciated for once. Her future was looking bright. Her heart fluttered when she saw him. She knew he was the man with whom she was going to spend the rest of her life.

"Now that you have the ring, what is your answer?" he asked, looking around to make sure no one was coming.

"It's been a yes for a long time, even before you asked. I knew I was going to say yes. I want to hug and kiss you right now, but I would lose my job, and we don't need that."

"Don't worry, my beautiful. Tomorrow I'm

going to make love to you with all my heart, mind, and body, and take my time appreciating all of you."

"I need to let you continue signing out before someone wonders why we're talking so long."

"See you tomorrow, beautiful. I love you!"

"I love you too, baby," she said as she walked away on cloud nine.

Juan moved on and showed his paperwork to sign out. As he was winding down with all of the signatures from the staff, he walked through the main corridor and saw Melanie with her belly showing. Her skin glowed, and a loving smile spread across her face when she spotted Juan coming her way. They knew they could not stop and talk for long, so Juan spoke as he passed her by.

"You're looking good, baby."

"Call me tonight. Me and the baby want to

talk to you," she responded, turning as she spoke, not caring if someone saw or heard what she said.

Since Juan was coming home the next day, she was going to be complete with him and her baby to be. Juan always felt something when he saw her, especially now with his baby inside of her. It was a baby boy, just like he wanted from the beginning.

He did not know how he was going to pull off the next day with both women planning to celebrate his release. He was now emotionally obligated to both of them, and he felt almost equally strong emotions for the both of them. He wanted to make them happy, and he wanted to give them both all of his love emotionally. His intent was not to play them or play with their emotions. He was really in love with the two of them, even though he did not understand that it was even possible until it happened to him. Dawn was his new fiancé, and Melanie was his baby mother-to-be. She also talked to him about marriage and having another baby with hopes of having a daughter, so they would have the perfect family. He always agreed, because he knew it would make her happy. Besides, a part of him thought having a baby girl would give balance to the family and relationship.

~ ~ ~

It was 5:30 p.m., and Deja was in the bathroom looking in the mirror. She was rubbing her belly and feeling the love inside of her. It was a baby girl—her princess-to-be.

Deja also felt the love, since she and Tom were getting married on Saturday, August 6. Tom hired a wedding planner to assist Deja with all of her likes, wants, and needs to make the day special. Her color theme was Tiffany blue, and her dress was customized by Donatella Versace. Tom was fitted for a tailored Sean Jean white suit with a Tiffany blue Sean Jean shirt, just as his bride had requested.

The guest list was full of members from both their families. As a gift to her, Tom paid for Tre Songz to sing on their special day. She was looking forward to this. The reception was also planned with DJ Large Flava on the tables. He knew to bring a mix of music to appease both families.

As Deja stood in thought, Tom walked into the bathroom and stared at his amazing wife-to-be.

"Hey, sexy lady, what you doing in here?"

"Rubbing our baby girl and thinking about our big day."

He came up behind her, kissed her neck, and wrapped his arms around her. He then joined in rubbing her belly.

"I can't wait until she comes, so we can spoil her."

"I know, papi! She's going to be a little diva." She paused and looked at him through the mirror. "Thank you for everything, baby. I love you for coming into my life and making this baby with me and making me the happiest woman in the world right now."

He took his hand and caressed through her long, silky hair before placing his lips close to her ear to speak.

"I thank you for believing that you deserve a love like this and staying around in my life. You made falling in love with you easy. That's how I knew you were the one and my wife-to-be."

He placed a passionate kiss to her ear and then her neck. She closed her eyes. Her heart felt good. She was comfortable in the arms of the man she loved with her all.

Their moment of love was interrupted when she felt the baby kick.

"Oh, the baby is kicking. Feel right here, papi!"

He placed his hand on her stomach and felt the baby's kick.

"That's my little angel inside of you."

"You know when she gets here you won't be getting too much loving because she'll have Mommy's attention."

"So, I guess now is the best time to make love to you before the baby gets here?"

"I want you now since we've been waiting a few weeks, but you have to wait until our wedding night when you make me Mrs. Jones," she said with a loving smile as she looked at him in the mirror.

He then placed more kisses to her neck and

ear, knowing her pleasure spots, but she resisted. She wanted to wait until their wedding day.

"Since this isn't working, let's go downstairs to feed you and the baby."

He tapped her on the bottom and felt the softness of her body. She looked over her shoulder at him with a salacious yet loving gaze.

~ ~ ~

Juan was in his cell under the covers at 9:40 p.m. talking on his cell phone with Melanie for the last hour and a half. She wanted to talk to him until the sun came up, if the battery would last that long or if they did not fall asleep in the process.

"Juan, our baby boy is moving inside of me. I wish you could feel him. He's going to be a little active guy and run all over the place."

He laughed thinking about chasing his son

around, playing with him, and being the dad, he wished he had.

"He's going to give both of us exercise."

"What type of sports do you think he'll want to play?"

"He might be a boxer or fight in the UFC."

"My baby isn't going to be in that stuff. I don't want him to get hurt."

"Mel, he won't be a baby then."

"He'll always be my baby, no matter how old he becomes."

He couldn't debate that; besides, she was right.

Juan was experiencing the excitement of being released. He knew he was not going to get much sleep, but he was more than ready to get out of here.

His cellmate, Puto, was going to get the cell phone, so he could keep in contact with him. He also wanted him to be able to reach out to his family in Mexico.

"Juan, do you want breakfast when you come home?"

"Only thing I'm going to be hungry for is your love."

She loved when he talked like this. She wanted him in her bed, like a soft cushion as he made love to her and then cuddled with her through the night, instead of having to rush away from one another as they did in the bathroom. She was looking forward to more intimate moments with him.

"We can do that, but our baby will need to eat when I get up. I was going to cook breakfast for us, so we can eat together, or lunch. Whatever you want, baby."

"I want to make you happy." She took his words to heart. A smile came across her face as she rubbed her belly. "Breakfast is good. I'm looking forward to this food being cooked with love, because it tastes better."

They continued to talk for another hour until the battery ran out, leaving them both anxious to see one another in the morning.

~ ~ ~

Deja was in a deep sleep at 1:37 a.m. snuggled with Tom at her side, with his arm lovingly wrapped around her.

She was having a dream about three men chasing someone. They did not see her, but she could see them. The person that was running was gunned down. She could not believe what she was seeing, even though she could not make out the faces of the men chasing the man or the man himself. The three men turned around and looked for witnesses. Her heart pounded as she tried to hide until they went away. They disappeared, but the person running was still on the ground not moving. She wanted to see who it was, so she walked up and stood over him. He was facedown, so she rolled him over. Right then she jumped up out of her sleep, with her heart and mind racing. She was breathing heavy and holding her stomach.

Her sudden movement woke Tom. He wanted to know if she and the baby were okay since she was rubbing her belly.

"Is our baby okay?"

"Yes!"

"Are you okay, babe?"

"I had a bad dream, that's all. I'll be fine. Go back to sleep."

She did not want to tell him what her dream was about, because it might upset him, even though he always said he did not believe in dreams, premonitions, or jinxes. However, she was a firm believer of this, but why have a dream like this? she wondered.

She laid her head back down, and her eyes stared up at the ceiling. She tried to figure out what the dream meant instead of misinterpreting what it really stood for.

A part of her became emotional as a tear slid down the side of her face. Being pregnant did not help; in fact, it only seemed to enhance the emotions and thoughts she was experiencing.

Chapter 14

*I*t was Friday, August 5, and Juan was in the reception area ready to leave. The corrections officer came out with his brand-new clothes that were sent to him as a gift.

"Dominguez, you can get dressed in room 5. I see you have some nice clothes and a Mercedes Benz limo out front waiting on you."

"It's about that time to live and celebrate the good life," Juan said, rubbing it in his face, knowing he was stuck working at the miserable job as a corrections officer.

Juan wondered which of his lovely ladies had sent the limo, since both of them were classy enough to do such a thing.

"I'm ready, CO," Juan said as he walked out

of the cell.

He was not even tired from staying up and writing a long love letter to Dawn. He knew he would be there when it arrived that Saturday morning. He thought it would be something she would always remember; besides, he did not have anything else to do.

"Follow me, Dominguez," the officer said, leading the way to the front door.

Juan felt his approaching freedom as each door opened. He did not look back. He was only looking forward to the future with the two women he loved.

The final door opened. The sun was shining bright, and the air, although the same on the other side of the locked doors, seemed to smell different. He appreciated it as he took a deep breath before walking toward the limo.

The chauffeur opened the door.

"Beverages are inside, sir," the chauffeur said before closing the door.

Juan got inside and appreciated the layout as well as the bottle of Moët on ice. It was early, but it was time for celebration.

The driver pulled off as Juan popped the bottle and poured himself a drink.

"I'm back, bitches!" he said before taking a sip. "To the good life and love," he added before downing the champagne and then filling his glass again.

He loved that he had outsmarted the system along with finding true love. On top of that, he managed to get $150,000. Life was definitely good right now.

The 19-inch flat-screen in the limo was located where the partition was. Videos were being played, which set the tone for the mood he was in. More champagne was downed, and minutes passed by before the limo came to a halt.

Juan was focused on the flat-screen until he heard the driver's door shut, which made him look out the window. They were stopped on a back road.

"What the fuck is this idiot doing?" Juan blurted out, feeling buzzed from the four glasses of champagne.

He turned to see a cargo van pull up behind the limo. When it came to a halt, three men jumped out with fully automatic weapons that they immediately unleashed onto the limo.

Bullets crashed into the limo, sounding off as each slug slammed into the frame.

Juan quickly reacted and kicked the 19-inch flat-screen TV and made his way into the front seat. There were no keys, so he hurried up and slipped out of the front of the limo but was spotted by one of the men.

Bullets raced through the air as they chased him down and slammed into his legs and back.

The three men rushed over to the downed Juan and turned him over, so they could see his face.

"*Tu chotta!!*"

When Juan saw their faces, he knew they were sent by the Mexican cartel who thought that he had snitched, even though he did not. They still had an FBI agent infiltrating their organization.

The Mexican hit men unleashed their slugs into Juan, filling his face and body and marring him to the fullest. The Mexicans then gunned down the chauffeur, so he could not be traced back to them. They raced back to the van and pulled off, leaving the dead bodies like a true cartel massacre.

~ ~ ~

Melanie was at her apartment in New Cumberland at 10:30 a.m. with breakfast on the stove. She wondered why it was taking Juan so long to get to her house. She called the prison an hour ago, and they said he already had left. She sat on the couch since it was close to the door, which was the same door she was waiting to see Juan walk through.

Fox News interrupted *The Maury Show*, which made her zoom in as the cameras showed a crime scene taped off. She knew right then someone was dead.

The caption underneath read: *Bloody massacre!* She turned the television up.

"These two murders were clearly out of hatred. They were massacred by the looks of the bodies lying on the other side of the tape. Local authorities say they have never seen anything like this. The driver was killed, as was the passenger, who appears to be Juan Dominguez. The authorities said they could not recognize his face, but he had a Camp Hill Prison ID on his possession. We've been informed that he was just released, so it's clear that someone was awaiting this day."

Melanie's heart was feeling as if she was stabbed with something hot and sharp. She fell off the couch onto the floor, especially when the corrections ID of him came across the screen. It was the same ID photo she had taken of him when he arrived at the prison.

"Nooooo! This can't be! This can't be happening to me!" she cried while holding on to her belly in the fetal position.

She yelled and cried out in deep emotional pain. Her pain was not just because she had lost the man she loved, but also because he was the father of her unborn child. She wanted to be with him. She wanted his love. She did not want to exist without his love and presence.

She was crying so hard that the baby started kicking, which reminded her there was a life on board—a life worth living for. It was a part of him that would live on, and a piece of him she could always love.

While she cried herself to sleep, over in Mechanicsburg, Tom walked into his bedroom carrying something to eat for Deja. She was crying heavily while watching the same news that Melanie had just seen. Tom looked at her and then the television. He set down the food and rushed over to his wife-to-be.

"What's wrong, baby?"

"He's dead. They killed him."

"Who's dead?"

"My ex, Juan. I knew this was going to

happen. I saw it in my dream the other night."

She felt somewhat guilty that she could not warn him, not that he would have wanted to hear anything from her.

She was not crying because she felt for him in a loving way. Her tears were because she was a compassionate person and she wished she could have prevented this.

Tom placed his arm around her with love to assure her that everything was going to be all right. He turned the television to another channel, so she did not have to see this graphic tableau.

"We have a baby in there, so stop crying. Everything is going to be okay. God doesn't make any mistakes. This was already written."

He rubbed her belly as she laid her head on him for comfort.

~ ~ ~

It was 12:07 p.m., and Dawn was at her place in Mechanicsburg crying for the last few hours, since she, too, had seen the news of Juan being massacred. She could not take her heart being ripped out as it was. She had made breakfast, and the table was set. That was just a fraction of what she had planned, and Breeana was looking forward to meeting him.

Juan wrote had written over one hundred letters. She had them all spread out and was reading them from beginning to end. She fell in love with him and cried for his love, his presence, and his touch, which was something she would never get again other than in a dream or with him in the afterlife. For the last thirty minutes, she had even contemplated drinking a bottle of cough syrup and taking a full pack of sleeping pills. She just wanted to be relieved from the immense emotional pain she was feeling.

She read another one of his letters, which only added fuel to the emotional fire. A part of her giggled in between the flowing tears and cries. Then she reached for the cough syrup and downed it within seconds. Before it could reach her system, she was popping pills one by one, tossing them into her mouth, chewing them up, and swallowing them.

She lay down on the floor on top of the spread-out letters.

"I love you, Juan. I love you so much. I'm coming to you, baby," she cried out sadly.

The cough syrup was rushing through her bloodstream making her eyes feel heavy. Her body also felt weighed down as the crushed sleeping pills took full effect.

She held onto a picture of Juan and stared at him until her eyelids closed. The picture slipped from her grasp. She was beyond a dream state; she was dying. While she fell into the abyss, a bright light came out of the darkness, followed by a voice.

"What are you doing?"

She wanted to say she loved him, but she was unable to speak.

"I love you, and I want to be with you. And in time we will be together, but not yet. Think about Breeana."

She heard Juan's voice and saw his face as she remembered him.

She even felt his touch and his kiss. It felt real.

"Now go home. Breeana is waiting on you."

As those words flowed from his mouth, she felt the love once more. This strong love gave her the strength to come back and to open her eyes.

When her eyes came open, she was in the

Holy Spirit Hospital, a place she had been for two days with IVs stuck in her arm.

The first face she saw was Breeana's on the edge of the bed. She looked like an angel smiling from ear to ear, seeing that her mommy was all better now.

The second face she saw was the neighbor's, who called 911 after hearing her screams and loud cries. She thought something was wrong—and it was.

The third face she saw was Melanie's, which was a face she did not expect to see.

"I bet you didn't expect to see me? You're still a good person, and we do work together. I'm glad you're okay," Melanie said.

Melanie did not know why Dawn had tried to commit suicide, but she honestly did feel sorry for her.

"Whenever you get better, I would like for

you to be the godmother to my baby boy."

Dawn broke a partial smile, even though her mouth was dry, and her lips felt chapped. She reached out and rubbed her motherly belly, remembering when she was pregnant.

"I take this as a yes?" Melanie said, placing her hand on Dawn's.

They looked at each other as if they had known the entire time they were sharing a piece of Juan, but they never wanted to really come out and say it. Right then, they both smiled. Melanie smiled because the baby boy inside of her was a piece of Juan. Dawn smiled because she was going to be a godmother, which also gave her the opportunity to have a piece of him.

Text Good2Go at 31996 to receive new release updates via text message.

PMC © 12172001-2-7-2011
A W.C. Holloway Story

To order books, please fill out the order form below:
To order films please go to www.good2gofilms.com

Name: __ _____

Address:_____

City: _____ State: _____ Zip Code: _____ _____

Phone:_____

Email:_____

Method of Payment: Check   VISA   MASTERCARD

Credit Card#:_ _____

Name as it appears on card: _____

Signature: _____

Item Name	Price	Qty	Amount
48 Hours to Die – Silk White	$14.99		
A Hustler's Dream - Ernest Morris	$14.99		
A Hustler's Dream 2 - Ernest Morris	$14.99		
A Thug's Devotion – J. L. Rose and J. M. McMillon	$14.99		
All Eyes on Tommy Gunz – Warren Holloway	$14.99		
Black Reign – Ernest Morris	$14.99		
Bloody Mayhem Down South – Trayvon Jackson	$14.99		
Bloody Mayhem Down South 2 – Trayvon Jackson	$14.99		
Business Is Business – Silk White	$14.99		
Business Is Business 2 – Silk White	$14.99		
Business Is Business 3 – Silk White	$14.99		
Childhood Sweethearts – Jacob Spears	$14.99		
Childhood Sweethearts 2 – Jacob Spears	$14.99		
Childhood Sweethearts 3 - Jacob Spears	$14.99		
Childhood Sweethearts 4 - Jacob Spears	$14.99		
Connected To The Plug – Dwan Marquis Williams	$14.99		
Connected To The Plug 2 – Dwan Marquis Williams	$14.99		
Connected To The Plug 3 – Dwan Williams	$14.99		
Deadly Reunion – Ernest Morris	$14.99		
Dream's Life – Assa Raymond Baker	$14.99		
Flipping Numbers – Ernest Morris	$14.99		
Flipping Numbers 2 – Ernest Morris	$14.99		
He Loves Me, He Loves You Not - Mychea	$14.99		
He Loves Me, He Loves You Not 2 - Mychea	$14.99		
He Loves Me, He Loves You Not 3 - Mychea	$14.99		
He Loves Me, He Loves You Not 4 – Mychea	$14.99		
He Loves Me, He Loves You Not 5 – Mychea	$14.99		

Lord of My Land – Jay Morrison	$14.99		
Lost and Turned Out – Ernest Morris	$14.99		
Love Hates Violence – De'Wayne Maris	$14.99		
Married To Da Streets – Silk White	$14.99		
M.E.R.C. - Make Every Rep Count Health and Fitness	$14.99		
Money Make Me Cum – Ernest Morris	$14.99		
My Besties – Asia Hill	$14.99		
My Besties 2 – Asia Hill	$14.99		
My Besties 3 – Asia Hill	$14.99		
My Besties 4 – Asia Hill	$14.99		
My Boyfriend's Wife - Mychea	$14.99		
My Boyfriend's Wife 2 – Mychea	$14.99		
My Brothers Envy – J. L. Rose	$14.99		
My Brothers Envy 2 – J. L. Rose	$14.99		
Naughty Housewives – Ernest Morris	$14.99		
Naughty Housewives 2 – Ernest Morris	$14.99		
Naughty Housewives 3 – Ernest Morris	$14.99		
Naughty Housewives 4 – Ernest Morris	$14.99		
Never Be The Same – Silk White	$14.99		
Shades of Revenge – Assa Raymond Baker	$14.99		
Slumped – Jason Brent	$14.99		
Someone's Gonna Get It – Mychea	$14.99		
Stranded – Silk White	$14.99		
Supreme & Justice – Ernest Morris	$14.99		
Supreme & Justice 2 – Ernest Morris	$14.99		
Supreme & Justice 3 – Ernest Morris	$14.99		
Tears of a Hustler - Silk White	$14.99		
Tears of a Hustler 2 - Silk White	$14.99		
Tears of a Hustler 3 - Silk White	$14.99		
Tears of a Hustler 4- Silk White	$14.99		
Tears of a Hustler 5 – Silk White	$14.99		
Tears of a Hustler 6 – Silk White	$14.99		
The Last Love Letter – Warren Holloway	$14.99		
The Last Love Letter 2 – Warren Holloway	$14.99		

The Panty Ripper - Reality Way	$14.99		
The Panty Ripper 3 – Reality Way	$14.99		
The Solution – Jay Morrison	$14.99		
The Teflon Queen – Silk White	$14.99		
The Teflon Queen 2 – Silk White	$14.99		
The Teflon Queen 3 – Silk White	$14.99		
The Teflon Queen 4 – Silk White	$14.99		
The Teflon Queen 5 – Silk White	$14.99		
The Teflon Queen 6 - Silk White	$14.99		
The Vacation – Silk White	$14.99		
Tied To A Boss - J.L. Rose	$14.99		
Tied To A Boss 2 - J.L. Rose	$14.99		
Tied To A Boss 3 - J.L. Rose	$14.99		
Tied To A Boss 4 - J.L. Rose	$14.99		
Tied To A Boss 5 - J.L. Rose	$14.99		
Time Is Money - Silk White	$14.99		
Tomorrow's Not Promised – Robert Torres	$14.99		
Tomorrow's Not Promised 2 – Robert Torres	$14.99		
Two Mask One Heart – Jacob Spears and Trayvon Jackson	$14.99		
Two Mask One Heart 2 – Jacob Spears and Trayvon Jackson	$14.99		
Two Mask One Heart 3 – Jacob Spears and Trayvon Jackson	$14.99		
Wrong Place Wrong Time – Silk White	$14.99		
Young Goonz – Reality Way	$14.99		
Subtotal:			
Tax:			
Shipping (Free) U.S. Media Mail:			
Total:			

Make Checks Payable To:
Good2Go Publishing
7311 W Glass Lane,
Laveen, AZ 85339

CPSIA information can be obtained
at www.ICGtesting.com
Printed in the USA
LVHW030953170919
631321LV00007B/197/P